MYSTERY
OF THE
PHANTOM
GOLD

AN
AMERICAN ADVENTURE
SERIES

MYSTERY
OF THE
PHANTOM
GOLD
LEE RODDY

BETHANY HOUSE PUBLISHERS
MINNEAPOLIS, MINNESOTA 55438

Published in association with the literary
agency of Alive Communications, P.O. Box
49068, Colorado Springs, Colorado 80949

Published by Bethany House Publishers
A Division of Bethany Fellowship, Inc.
6820 Auto Club Road, Minneapolis, Minnesota 55438

Printed in the United States of America

Library of Congress Cataloging-in-Publication Data

Mystery of the phantom gold / Lee Roddy.
    p. cm. — (An American adventure ; bk. 7)
    Summary: Hildy Corrigan is thrust into unexpected jeopardy and learns
a valuable lesson about God when she tries to help her benefactor learn
who is stealing gold from his mine in California's historic Mother Lode.

    [1. Mystery and detective stories. 2. Gold mines and mining—Fic-
tion. 3. Christian life—Fiction.]
I. Title. II. Series: Roddy, Lee, 1921–   American adventure ; bk. 7.
PZ7.R6Mym   1991
[Fic]—dc20   91–20272
                                                      CIP
ISBN 1–55661-210-9   AC

To
the memory of

Neva D. (Gordon) Roddy,

married 55 years
and mother of 10,
all living,
of which I'm the oldest

LEE RODDY is a bestselling author and motivational speaker. Many of his over 50 books, such as *Grizzly Adams*, *Jesus*, *The Lincoln Conspiracy*, the *D. J. Dillon Adventure Series*, and the *Ladd Family Adventures* have been bestsellers, television programs, book club selections or have received special recognition. All of his books support traditional moral, spiritual, and family values.

CONTENTS

CHAPTER ONE

STRANGER'S GOLD

Tuesday Noon

Something was wrong. Hildy Corrigan sensed that the moment she and her friend Spud approached Lone River's only bank that noon in early October. The two-story yellow-brick structure with the clock on top was located at the corner of Main and Broadway. This was the principal intersection in the small California agricultural community of Lone River.

Spud, wearing tennis shoes, rumpled corduroy pants, and a white shirt open at the neck with sleeves rolled up above the elbow, reached out to open the heavy mahogany door. A tall, wiry man in his early twenties rushed from inside the bank, rudely pushed past the boy and girl, glanced around nervously, then turned sharply to the right and walked rapidly away down Main Street.

It happened fast, barely giving the blue-eyed twelve-year-old girl a glimpse of a man about six feet tall with a long, slender face and scraggly blond moustache. He hurried down the sidewalk carrying a small wooden box under his left arm.

Hildy hesitated before the bank door, which Spud still held open. She started to enter, then swiveled her head for another look at the stranger. She moved so quickly that her waist-length brown braids swung against Spud. He asked, "What's the matter?"

"I don't know. I just had the strangest feeling—"

She was interrupted by a small, dapper man in a dark blue business suit with a gold watch chain stretched across his vest. He rushed from inside the bank to stop just inside the door which Spud still held open.

"Hildy! Spud!" Matthew Farnham, the bank president, greeted them in a low, excited voice. "Did you see the man who just left here?"

When Hildy and Spud nodded, Mr. Farnham exclaimed, "Follow him! Find out where he goes! If he gets in a car, get the license number. But don't let him see you. Come back as soon as you can!"

"What's going on?" Spud asked.

"Tell you later. Hurry, don't lose him! But be careful!" The banker gently but firmly shoved the two outside and quickly closed the door behind them.

For a moment Hildy and Spud stared at each other in bewilderment. Then they turned and hurried after the stranger, who was about half a block ahead.

Hildy asked, "I wonder what he did to upset Mr. Farnham?"

Spud shoved the goggles higher up on top of the aviator cap he always wore in honor of his hero, Charles A. Lindbergh, who had flown the Atlantic alone in a single-engine airplane seven years before. Reddish hair curled out from under Spud's cap.

"Well," he mused, "he didn't rob the bank or Mr. Farnham would've called for the police."

"Then why did he tell us to be careful and not let that man know we're following him?"

Spud looked at Hildy with green eyes that seemed just right for his heavily freckled face and hands. "Guess we'll have to wait until we find out where he goes and report back to Mr. Farnham."

Hildy almost ran to keep up with Spud. She wore a rose-and-beige flowered cotton dress with a lace-edged, white V-neck collar she'd helped her stepmother make. The hem fell about two inches below Hildy's knees, so she bent and lifted it slightly to more easily match Spud's long stride.

They hurried past the haberdashery and dime store. Each displayed the Blue Eagle of President Roosevelt's NRA with the slogan, "We do our part." The next three stores were boarded up because this was 1934, the fifth year of the Depression, and hard times were everywhere.

Hildy's blue eyes studied the stranger ahead. He wore a checkered cap, workingman's pants, shirt and boots. He held the box against his body as though it were important.

"There's something scary about that man," Hildy said. "I can't explain it, but I had the strangest feeling when I first saw him." When Spud didn't answer, Hildy added anxiously, "I sure hope this doesn't take long. We had only twenty minutes to get to the bank, get your papers signed, and get back to school."

Spud turned to look back at the huge clock on top of the bank building. "We've still got fifteen minutes."

"Look!" Hildy cried. "He's turning the corner by the hardware store onto Sycamore Street."

Spud warned, "When we get there, let's be careful. Don't go around the corner too fast. We don't want to bump into him or do anything to make him suspicious."

Hildy nodded and slowed to match Spud's pace. They made a wide swing around the corner. Hildy sighed with relief to see that the stranger was still hurrying along ahead of them. Suddenly he stopped and turned at right angles.

Hildy said under her breath, "He's either looking in that store window, or he's watching out of the corner of his eye to see if we're following him."

"Quick! Look in this window but try to watch him in the reflection," Spud suggested.

Hildy obeyed, glad to stop, because she'd gone barefoot all summer, and her feet weren't yet used to the white ankle socks and sturdy new dusty-beige oxfords.

The hardware store's plate-glass panel was set in at an angle so it reflected the stranger. Spud whispered, "I can see his eyes. Now I'm sure that he's checking to see if anybody's following him."

"You think he knows that's what we're doing? I mean, maybe he recognized us from when he almost bumped into me at the bank door."

"I don't know, but let's try not to look suspicious. Point to something inside the window in case he's really watching us."

Hildy refocused her eyes from the reflection to the display inside. She spotted a wooden washing machine without a wringer. Hildy pointed and raised her voice a little louder than necessary, in case the stranger could hear. "I wish my stepmother could have one of those instead of having to use a washboard and tubs like my mother did."

Spud played along, raising his voice a bit. "But it doesn't have a wringer. Still, it's only $15.95. That new electric one next to it, with a wringer, costs $61."

"But we don't have electricity at our place," Hildy reminded him. She lowered her voice and refocused on the stranger's reflection in the window. "Why should he be checking to see if he is being followed, unless he did something wrong?"

Spud shrugged. "I don't know. Maybe it has something to do with that box he's carrying. Hey, there he goes!"

Hildy watched the stranger's reflection in the glass. He hurried to the curb and slid into the passenger side of a cream-colored 1929 Model-A coupe with a rumble seat.

Still pretending to look into the store window, Hildy whispered, "Can you see who's driving?"

"No, the sun's reflecting off the windshield so I can't see anything except that he's wearing a black cowboy hat."

"We've got to get the license number, but it's backward in the reflection, like a mirror. We'll have to turn around to read it."

"Okay. Let's walk past the car but don't look at it. Wait'll the driver backs out. It'll be easier to see the rear plate then."

Hildy and Spud turned away from the window and casually strolled down the sidewalk. Hildy watched out of the corner of her eye as the Model A started up. The driver waited to let a horse and buggy pass. The stranger rolled down his window and looked hard at Hildy and Spud.

"I think he's suspicious," Hildy whispered as they drew even with the vehicle.

"Just act naturally," Spud said hoarsely above the clip-clop of the passing horse's hooves. "Don't look at them. Just keep walking."

The car backed up, then headed north along Sycamore, making the rear plate easy to read. "I've got it!" Hildy exclaimed as the car turned east at the corner.

"Me, too! Come on!" Spud led the run back to the bank. They arrived breathless and entered the bank. Suddenly Spud grabbed Hildy's arm. "Don't look now," he exclaimed, looking through the large window, "but there's that car again! They've followed us, meaning they really are suspicious."

"You think they saw us come in here?"

"No doubt about it. Boy, I sure hope we aren't in any danger—especially when we don't even know what's going on!"

The banker, Matthew Farnham, opened the inside office door and motioned for Hildy and Spud to enter his private office.

Anxious and a little concerned, Hildy hurried past two women customers at the cashier's window, where a bald man waited on them.

"Well?" the banker asked breathlessly as he closed the heavy oak door behind Hildy and Spud. He motioned them to seats in front of his glistening walnut desk, then sat down himself. "Where did he go?"

After quickly relating what they saw, Hildy asked, "What's this all about?"

For a moment, the banker hesitated. Then he lowered his voice and leaned across the desk. "He's stealing from my gold mine," the banker said softly.

"Gold mine?" Hildy exclaimed in surprise.

"Shh! Keep your voice down!" Mr. Farnham warned.

Spud whispered, "I didn't know you had a gold mine."

"Most people don't," the banker whispered back. "It's up in the Mother Lode Country. One of my private investments."

Hildy frowned. "How do you know he's stealing your gold?"

The banker relaxed slightly and leaned back. He laced his fingers behind his head, allowing his suit coat to fall open. Sunlight streaming through the window flashed off the gold watch chain looped across his vest.

He explained, "Most people don't know it, but each hardrock mine in the Mother Lode produces gold that's distinctive from any other mine. That's true even of mines in the same area. The gold from each mine is recognizable, just as human fingerprints differ from one person to another."

Spud said, "I read that someplace, but I didn't believe it."

"It's true," the banker assured him. "Oh, not just anybody off the streets could see the difference. But a geologist can, and one taught me how to recognize the gold from the Shasta Daisy. That's the name of my mine."

Hildy persisted, "But how did that man—?"

"I'm coming to that," the banker said. "That man you kids followed came in here a while ago and said he wanted to rent a safe-deposit box. He was all excited and became really upset when the box he carried in fell off my desk and a corner of the lid popped up. Two pieces of quartz slid across the floor.

"Well, you never saw a man scramble so fast to retrieve something! I tried to help by picking up one piece, and that's when I got a good look at it. There's no doubt. That's gold from my mine. It's being highgraded."

"What's that mean?" Hildy asked.

The banker explained, "That's a term meaning that highgrade gold—that which is worth more—is being stolen."

"Stolen?" Hildy exclaimed.

Mr. Farnham nodded vigorously. "Absolutely!"

Spud asked, "What'd you do when you realized that man was highgrading your gold?"

"I managed to keep a straight face, but he became flustered and wouldn't rent the safe-deposit box. He picked up his wooden box and left. While he was doing that, I was trying hard to think what to do. I couldn't call the police, because I've got to know first how the gold's being smuggled out of the mine.

"Other people would have to be involved, too, and I need to know who they are so I can stop the stealing. Just as he was going out the door, you two walked in, and you know the rest. Thanks very much for your help."

Hildy said, "It was nothing. But I don't understand—"

Spud interrupted. "We'd like to hear more, but we've got to get back. Because this is my first day at school, the office gave me a paper saying that you're acting as my temporary guardian." He produced a paper from his right hip pocket. "Sign at the X on the bottom, please."

"Gladly." The banker picked up a thick fountain pen, uncapped it, and scribbled his name. "I hope your father sends the documents soon that will make this a permanent arrangement. Then he won't ever be able to beat you again." Mr. Farnham blotted the ink and handed the paper back.

"Thanks," Spud said, standing up.

Hildy also stood. "I sure hope that license plate number will help you catch whoever's stealing your gold, Mr. Farnham."

"While you two were following the stranger, I decided to call Ben Strong and ask him to investigate the case for me."

Hildy and Spud nodded. Brother Ben was a Civil War Veteran, former U.S. Marshal and Texas Ranger, now nearly eighty-six years old and living in Lone River.

It was getting close to one o'clock, so Hildy and Spud said hurried goodbyes and started walking rapidly west, toward the school grounds. They had barely passed the haberdasher's when a tremendous air horn blasted the calm.

Hildy jumped, then exclaimed, "I'll never get used to that noise!" The horn stood atop a metal tower on the city hall roof three blocks south of Main Street. The horn blew at nine o'clock in the morning, at twelve o'clock noon, and five o'clock in the afternoon. It was also used to call volunteer firemen.

Spud swiveled his head, studying the sky in all directions. "Since it's blowing this time of day, there's got to be a fire. Listen. The number of blasts tells the firemen where the fire is."

Hildy and Spud stopped and listened. "Five blasts," Hildy said when there was a pause. The horn sounded twice more before pausing again. "Five and two. Wonder what part of the town that's in?"

"We'll soon find out," Spud said, turning to look toward city hall. "I can hear fire engines. Sounds as if they're coming this way."

Moments later, two ancient red Liberty pumpers, left over from the Great War sixteen years before, thundered into view. They passed Hildy and Spud, heading west along Main Street. A string of volunteer firemen followed in their own cars.

"Must be near the school," Hildy mused. "But I don't see any smoke."

"Come on!" Spud cried, breaking into a run. "Let's find out."

Not much in the way of excitement happened in Lone River, so everyone who could, ran or drove after the fire engines and their volunteers. Hildy ran hard, keeping pace with Spud.

"The trucks are pulling up in front of the school!" Spud exclaimed.

Hildy glanced hurriedly at the two-story red-brick Northside Grammar School for seventh and eighth graders. "I still don't see any smoke. But look at all the kids running away from the building! Teachers, too!"

The fire truck stopped as Hildy and Spud approached on a dead run. One volunteer in a red fireman's hat jumped off the back of the truck and dashed toward Hildy, Spud, and the crowd of other curious people approaching the site. "Get back!" the fireman yelled. "There's a gas leak! The whole building could blow up!"

CHAPTER
TWO

A SURPRISE VISITOR

Tuesday Afternoon

The volunteer fireman quickly herded Hildy, Spud, and other students with their teachers across the dirt schoolyard to the relative safety of the bus barns. They all stood at the farthest point from the old red-brick building. Everyone chattered excitedly about the gas leak, which one teacher said was in the basement.

Hildy, a country girl without electric lights or indoor plumbing at home, didn't know about natural gas. However, her friend Spud was knowledgeable about many things, so she turned to him.

"How could gas blow up our school?" she asked.

Spud shoved his aviator cap up from his freckled forehead so that curly reddish locks escaped. "Natural gas is heavy, so when it escapes, it settles down, sort of pooling in the air of a basement, for example. Then all it takes is a spark, match or some other open flame—and boom!"

A very thin girl in a black dress, which had obviously been cut down from a woman's garment, overheard Spud and moved closer. Like Spud, Gladys Cassell was spending her first day in Hildy's seventh-grade class.

She asked in a frightened voice, "Do you think there's any real danger?" She nodded her head of short dark hair to indicate the red-brick school building.

"I hope not," Spud said honestly.

Hildy reached out impulsively and touched the new girl's bare forearm. "Don't worry! It'll be okay."

Hildy felt sorry for Gladys, a Dust Bowl refugee, whose sad brown eyes reflected the hardships she had known too well in her twelve years of life. Hildy was also a refugee, but she had an inner strength of faith that helped her deal with hardships.

Spud continued as other students clustered around: "I remember reading about a gas leak in the basement of one school. When it exploded, the entire building was destroyed, and some kids were killed."

Hildy gave him a warning glance just as Ruby Konning, her thirteen-year-old tomboy cousin, pushed her way through the excited crowd of students. Her hazel eyes, wide with fright, focused on Hildy.

Ruby exclaimed in her Ozark Mountain accent, "Didja hear? We cud be blowed sky high!"

Hildy suspected that her cousin sometimes deliberately used poor English to show how little she cared about other people's opinions.

Ruby and Spud didn't get along well, so neither spoke nor seemed to notice the other's presence.

"We'll be just fine!" Hildy said soothingly. She wanted to tell what had happened at the bank, so she took Ruby by the hand. "Come away from all this noise."

As the cousins turned away, Hildy caught a glimpse of Gladys' doleful face. For a moment, Hildy was tempted to invite the lonesome new girl to join them. But Hildy knew that it wouldn't be proper to share with Gladys the events involving the stolen gold.

"Excuse us," Hildy said. "We'll be right back."

When they were at the end of the school grounds beyond the bus sheds, Hildy quickly told Ruby about the stranger and the stolen gold. She had just finished her account and Ruby started to ask a question when Mr. Ebenezer Wiley, the school principal, walked across the empty school grounds. He was bald and of medium build, wearing a well-worn brown suit.

He looked over the top of gold-colored, wire-rimmed glasses, cupped his hands, and called for attention. When the crowd was silent, he said, "The fire chief has advised that it will take some time to find the leak. So in the interest of safety, school is dismissed for the day."

A chorus of ragged cheers erupted from the crowd. The principal again waited for quiet, then continued: "All those who ride buses are to remain here by the sheds until the drivers are ready. All students who walk to school are to leave the grounds immediately for your homes. Everyone listen to the radio station for information on whether school will resume tomorrow."

A short time later everyone except Hildy was singing or shouting joyfully as the old high-topped red school bus, affectionately known as *The Sardine Can*, bounced along the graveled country road. Hildy and Ruby had their heads together discussing details of Hildy and Spud's experience at the bank.

Ruby asked softly, "Ye reckon yo're in danger from them two strangers?"

"I hope not. But if I am, so's Spud."

Ruby dismissed the boy with an impatient wave of her hand. "Shore wish we'uns was jist a little bit as rich as Mr. Farnham! 'Course, he's the richest man in town."

"He's also one of the nicest," Hildy answered. "So's his wife and kids. You know that."

The cousins worked part-time for Mrs. Farnham, a polio victim confined to a wheelchair. Spud, a runaway from his drunken father, had recently started living with the Farnhams and their two little children.

Ruby's voice rose slightly, and her brown eyes opened wide. "Hey, I jist got me an idee! Wouldn't it be a powerful lot of fun if'n ye and me could he'p ketch them crooks who are stealin' the gold?"

"Shh!" Hildy glanced anxiously around, realizing the bus had stopped but nobody was getting off. Everyone had grown quiet and seemed to be staring at her. Even the bus driver regarded her in the big rearview mirror.

Ruby gave her a nudge. "He's a-waitin' fer ye. This is yore stop. Yore new house."

Embarrassed at having forgotten that her family had moved over the weekend, Hildy scrambled forward, smiling at Spud as she passed. She stepped down from the bus onto the dirt shoulder of the road and looked toward the house her father had just rented for $15 a month.

She stood staring thoughtfully at it as the bus pulled away, its tires throwing gravel from the roadway. The house squatted like an ugly, black bug a quarter-mile back off the county road about three miles from town. The nearest neighbor was a half-mile away.

This was the third place Hildy and her family had lived in since arriving in California three months before. At first they had lived in a used tent beside the river, like many other Midwestern and Southern refugees fleeing the Dust Bowl or the Depression in general. Hard times had followed most of the refugees to the promised land of California, but at least here there was hope.

The Corrigans had lived in one end of a barn for a couple of months. Now they had a tarpaper shack. It took the name from the rolls of black roofing paper that had been used to cover the outside of the frame dwelling.

It had been made of green lumber by someone who was obviously not a skilled carpenter. The wood had dried in the blistering summer sun so that some boards had pulled apart. Hildy's footloose cowboy father, Joe Corrigan, had jokingly said he could throw his quarter horse through the cracks and never touch a hair on the animal. Hildy knew that was an exaggeration, but it was certain that wasps and dirt daubers had gotten into Hildy's bedroom and built nests in the ceiling.

Still, it was nicer than the sharecropper's cabin in which Hildy had been born. Running water had been piped from the tankhouse to the lean-to kitchen. There was no other indoor plumbing, so the weathered outhouse with the crescent moon cut in the door stood several yards downwind from the three-room house with the added-on kitchen and extra bedroom. Hildy had grown up with kerosene lamps, so she didn't mind not having electric lights.

But Hildy was a dreamer. Her dream was that someday her family would own a "forever" home where they'd never have to move again. Still, this poor shelter, an unsightly scab on a lonely, desolate country hill surrounded by windblown dry grass, was a step up from anything she had yet known.

Hildy lifted the metal hoop off the gate post and carefully stepped through the opening, watching that the rusted barbed wire didn't snag her homemade school dress. She closed the gate and hurried down the deeply rutted road, her new shoes kicking up dust. The October wind, hinting at the coming winter, caught the dust and whirled it away to become a part of the dreary, treeless landscape.

Hildy tried to be cheerful about the progress her family had made. She walked along, watching the sunlight reflect off her shiny lunch pail, which once had been a lard bucket.

"Molly," she called as she passed the last of the sun-browned weeds near the shack. "I'm home."

When her stepmother didn't answer, Hildy bounced up the high screened-in front porch and into the combination living and dining room. The print in the linoleum was worn and faded, and the couch was broken down, with the springs sticking up from one cushion. There were two small, homemade pine tables. One held a purple glass vase; the other supported an open black leather-bound Bible.

Hildy glanced into the bedroom on the right to see her seventeen-month-old baby brother sleeping in a crib made of a lug box lined with old clothes. Lug boxes, which once held fruit or vegetable produce, were always put to good use.

She set her lunch bucket on the dining table and stepped into the lean-to kitchen. Two old hickory chairs had been turned down so their sturdy backs rested on lug boxes. Both chairs supported galvanized washtubs.

Hildy's stepmother, Molly, knelt on the cracked floor, her back to Hildy, vigorously scrubbing on a washboard placed upright in the first tub.

Hildy's mouth tightened in a hard, grim line as she remembered her first mother doing the same thing in a sharecropper's cabin. Hildy often wondered if her mother's early death had been hastened by scrubbing clothes for her five girls.

Even though other women warned her not to, Elizabeth Corrigan had been on her knees over a washboard shortly before her only son was born. She died a year ago in May when Joey entered the world.

Hildy's lips moved in a quick, silent prayer: *Lord, Molly needs a washing machine so she won't die like Mom did.*

Molly, a woman in her middle thirties, looked up suddenly. "Hildy, you startled me! I didn't hear you come in." With the back of a sudsy hand, she brushed loose strands of hair away from her eyes. Hildy saw a few strands of gray among the light brown ones.

"I'm sorry," Hildy said, wrinkling her nose at the smell of the hot soapy water. "School let out early. I'll go change clothes and then finish the washing. You sit and rest, okay?"

"What happened that they sent you home this time of day?" Molly asked, slowly rising to her feet and stretching.

Hildy explained quickly, then hurried into the small, cramped bedroom that opened off the kitchen. She shared it with her ten-year-old sister, Elizabeth. Both slept on old army cots, but it was far better than the pallets of old clothes, coats, and blankets they'd had at the barn-house. Three younger sisters shared the middle bedroom, while baby Joey slept in a corner of the front bedroom with his parents.

A few minutes later, barefoot and wearing a faded housedress, Hildy knelt before the tub. Her knees, scarred from picking cotton at the age of five, hurt when she kneeled, but Hildy ignored the discomfort. She lifted a waterlogged pair of her father's heavy work pants and began rubbing them on the washboard. Then she told Molly about the bank incident.

Molly stood by the kitchen stove and poured bluing into a copper boiler that covered two burners. Then she picked up a broom handle to stir the bleach-like liquid through the boiling water, and to poke the clothes beneath the surface.

She said, "I wonder how Brother Ben will go about figuring out how Mr. Farnham's gold is being stolen. I know he's had a great career as a lawman, but he's well up in years now. I'd guess he'll need help."

"Wish I could help!" Hildy said fervently. "I keep recalling that funny feeling I had when I first saw that stranger with the gold." She stopped scrubbing a pair of her father's work socks, wrung them, and tossed them into the other tub to rinse. "I'd do anything to help Mr. Farnham, because he's done so much for us."

Molly turned around. "I know you would."

"I read in the paper the other day that President Roosevelt said all gold has to be sold to the government for $35 an ounce. But times are so hard I guess some men would risk going to jail for not complying."

"I guess so, although I can't imagine your father stealing. Still, with millions of men out of work, some must get pretty desperate."

She added, "Your father's lucky to be working, even though it means riding the range from sunup to sundown six days a week for a mere $15."

"That means Daddy has to work more than two weeks to earn as much as one ounce of gold is worth."

Molly nodded, bending over the rinse tub. "If you'll give me a hand wringing these out, we can get them on the line to dry before your sisters get home."

Soon the old, mostly patched clothes were flapping in the

breeze. Each garment was held in place on the rope line by wooden pins that resembled a row of tiny-headed, wingless birds. Hildy raised the pole in the middle to lift the line up so the trailing clothes were well above the dusty ground.

Molly picked up the empty clothes basket and headed for the house. Hildy fell into step beside her, then stopped and turned around. She shaded her eyes against the glare of the afternoon sun so she could see the distant barbed-wire gate. "That looks like Brother Ben's car," she announced.

The big 1929 Packard 645 Victoria swept grandly up the rutted driveway with a flash of bright yellow body paint and brown trim, wide white sidewall tires, and glistening chrome radiator, hood ornament, and triple headlights.

Hildy and Molly hurried to the driver's side and bent their heads to peer under the tan canvas top and through the open window.

After brief greetings, the tall, straight-backed driver gave his white walrus moustache a flip with the back of his right finger and looked at Hildy. He asked in his soft drawl, "Did you tell Molly what happened at the bank this morning?" When Hildy nodded, the old ranger added, "Matt asked me to help find the men who are stealing his gold."

Hildy replied, "He told Spud and me he was going to have you do that."

"I'll need a couple of good men," the old ranger continued. "I'm going to ask Ruby's father."

Nate Konning was an itinerant preacher temporarily working part-time on a nearby ranch.

"He's a good man," Molly said, approving.

Ben added, "Molly, Matt said he'd speak to the Woods brothers where your husband works, because I need him to help on this case, too."

Hildy said wistfully, "Wish I could help!"

The old man smiled wanly. "You might just get your wish, young lady!"

CHAPTER
THREE
—

SHOCKING NEWS

Tuesday Evening & Wednesday Morning

W hat?" Hildy asked, drawing back in surprise.
The old ranger stepped from the Packard into the dusty yard. He stood about six-four but looked taller in his highly polished cowboy boots and ten-gallon hat.

"Yup!" he assured her. "Matt wants me to use my experience as an officer of the law to investigate this case, and I'll need your help. That is, if your stepmother doesn't mind?" He turned questioning eyes on Molly and gave her the barest hint of a courtly bow.

"Come inside," Molly replied, "and we'll talk."

Inside the tarpaper shack, Molly took Ben's big white hat and hung it on a spike by the front door. She motioned for the guest to seat himself on the couch at the far end from the broken spring.

"As you know, Brother Ben," she said, "we just moved in over the weekend. We didn't bring any furniture with us to California, and Joe's not had time or money to buy any, so we're making do with what the landlord left in this house."

"This is real nice for a man like me," Ben said with a smile, "who spent his life on the range, squatting on his boot heels when he wasn't in the saddle."

Molly smiled her thanks at the old gentleman's gallantry. She sat down beside him, being careful to avoid the broken spring. "Hildy," she said, "please run outside and bring in an empty lug box to sit on."

"Okay, but don't say anything interesting until I get back." Hildy was filled with curiosity about how Brother Ben needed her help in catching the gold thieves.

She dashed out and returned with the empty lug box. She placed it directly in front of her stepmother and their guest.

"Now," Hildy prompted, "tell me what you meant about how I might get my wish."

"You said you've already told Molly about the adventure you and Spud had at Matt Farnham's bank."

"Yes, and I also told Ruby. Should I not have said anything?"

"No, it's fine to have told Molly and Ruby. I just hope you didn't tell anyone else."

Relieved, Hildy shook her head. "I didn't."

"So now," the old man said, "you both pretty well know everything except the possible motive for the highgrading."

Molly smiled. "It has to be for the money. I was telling Hildy just a while ago that my husband works a whole week for $15. He'd have to work more than two weeks to make the $35 that an ounce of gold brings from the government."

A slow grin spread over the guest's weathered face. "It's more than money in this case, Molly. It's greed. You see, in the United States, gold must be sold to the government for the fixed price you mention. However, on the world market, that same ounce of gold is worth $700."

"Seven hundred dollars for one ounce?" Hildy exclaimed.

Ben nodded. "Yup! And that's for a troy ounce—just twelve ounces to a pound. That's how gold is measured, instead of the standard sixteen ounces to a pound."

Hildy figured it quickly in her head. "Let's see: 12 ounces times $700 . . . that's $8400!"

"Oh, my stars!" Molly exclaimed. "Awhile ago I said to Hildy that Mr. Farnham must not have told her everything. Now I understand what he didn't say, and why."

Ben gave his white walrus moustache a flip with the back of his right forefinger. "Matt told me that while Hildy and Spud were following the stranger, he realized that even if they got the car's license number, and he found out through Sacramento who owned it, it would be just the tip of the iceberg.

"You see, both he and I already knew that millions of dollars in gold is highgraded each year," Ben continued. "The thieves are almost never caught. Even when they are, there's no court record that I've ever heard about in which the highgraders went to jail. The crime is just too common. Even a jury would probably be made up of those who'd done the same thing at some time or other."

Molly exclaimed, "Surely you're not suggesting that Mr. Farnham's going to let those men get away with stealing his gold?"

"No, he and I would both like to see them behind bars. However, Matt's first objective is to find out who's stealing from his mine, how the gold is smuggled from deep underground, and who handles it from there until it reaches Mexico."

"Mexico?" Molly repeated.

"That's the most likely way to get the gold started into the world market," Ben explained. "Once we know who's responsible and how it's done, maybe we can stop it. Then we'll see if there's enough evidence to bring those men to trial."

Molly asked, "How does Hildy fit into all this?"

"If you and Joe agree to it, I'd like to have Hildy go up to Quartz City in Gold County with me. She could get acquainted with some of the kids whose fathers work in the mines. Maybe Hildy could pick up some bits of information that'd be helpful to me in this case."

Molly frowned thoughtfully. "Isn't that dangerous?"

"I don't think so. The highgraders wouldn't suspect a young girl."

Hildy asked, "What about the stranger Spud and I followed? He and the man driving the Model A circled back to the bank and saw us enter. I think they're suspicious of us, so do you think we'll run into either of those men?"

"It's possible, because they undoubtedly work around Matt's mine," Ben admitted. "But why would they want to hurt either of you?"

"Maybe because we could identify them—or at least the one we followed."

"I don't think so. Remember what I said about there being no court convictions of highgraders? I think they'll be pretty fearless."

Hildy was satisfied, then remembered something. "Oh, I can't go because of school!"

The old ranger smiled, "I haven't told you yet, but I ran into the fire chief at the cafe this morning. He said that they've turned off the gas at the school, but it'll take several days for the part to come so the leak can be repaired. School's closed until then."

Hildy, always in search of excitement, leaped up from the lug box. "Oh, Molly, may I go? Please?"

"We'll have to wait and see what your father says when he gets home."

It was after dark, as usual, when the lights from Joe Corrigan's long Rickenbacker hit the windows of the tarpaper shack. Hildy's four little sisters and baby brother were already asleep; only Hildy and her stepmother were still up when Joe entered.

His deeply tanned face showed his weariness. He barely spoke, but removed his Western hat and dropped it on the spike by the door. His face was dark from the sun except for the pale white band on his forehead where the hat usually rested. His blue eyes were bloodshot, and his stubbly black beard was grimy from riding the dust behind half-wild cattle all day. He sank with a tired sigh onto the lug box and removed his scuffed cowboy boots. In stocking feet, he padded into the kitchen and washed up at the sink.

It took all of Hildy's willpower to wait to tell her father the

news until she and Molly had served him a plate of boiled po-
tatoes and country gravy, which had been kept hot on the back
of the wood-burning stove. When her father started eating,
Hildy sat down on a hickory chair opposite him. She looked
past the kerosene lamp to where he sat on the other side of the
table with its cracked and faded oilcloth covering.

Molly, standing behind her husband's chair, lightly rested
her red, chapped hands on his broad shoulders. "Joe," she began quietly, "Brother Ben was by earlier."

Her husband swallowed a piece of biscuit. "Then you must
know the banker asked my boss to let me have a few days off
to help Ben find those men who are stealing the gold."

"He told us that was a possibility," Molly replied.

Joe continued, "You also must know that Ben wants Nate to
help too."

Molly said, "Yes, but after Ben had gone, I got to thinking
about Ruby. Nate won't go off and leave her alone."

Joe pushed his plate back. "You're right. She's going along
with us."

"With us?" Hildy asked a little breathlessly.

"If Molly can spare you, you're going too," her father said.

Hildy almost jumped up and down with excitement, but she
glanced at her stepmother and waited.

Molly asked, "Joe, don't you think it'll be too dangerous?
Not just for Hildy and Ruby, but for you and Nate."

Hildy's father leaned back in his chair so it rested only on the
two back legs. "There's a risk in everything, from going out in
traffic to herding cattle all day."

Hildy frowned. "Are you saying I can go?"

Her father brought the chair back to all four legs and leaned
across the table to take her small hands in his rough, calloused
ones. He explained, "There's probably a greater risk anytime
gold is involved. However, I've talked to Nate and Ben, and we
feel there shouldn't be any danger if everyone's careful. You see,
all any of us has to do is keep our eyes and ears open and our
mouths shut. Besides, Matt said he'd pay $5 a day per man, plus

the $3.50 or so Nate and I will earn in the mine."

Molly let out a slow breath. "That's $8.50 a day—more than half what you're making in six days as a rider!"

"And Ben said Matt would give the girls a little something, plus pay expenses for all of us."

Hildy knew that Ruby wanted a $10 used bike, and Hildy wanted to buy a $15 wooden washing machine for her step-mother. Hildy wondered if the banker would pay anywhere near that amount to Ruby and her if they helped catch the high-graders.

Joe continued, "So, Molly, what do you say? Can you spare Hildy and me for a few days?"

Hildy held her breath while her stepmother hesitated, then nodded. "Elizabeth's old enough to fill in for her big sister until you get back," Molly said.

"Good!" her husband replied, releasing Hildy's hands and standing up. "Now let's get some sleep. We'll have to get up early, because Ben'll be here right after sunup to take us to Quartz City in Gold County."

Hildy was still excited the next morning when the big Pack-ard rolled up to the tarpaper shack. Spud was in the front seat. Ruby and her father were in the back. After Joe and Ben stored the Corrigans' meager belongings in the small trunk, Hildy sat in back with her cousin and uncle while Joe Corrigan sat up front, with Spud between him and the old ranger.

"Now," Ben began, raising his voice so all could hear, "here's the plan. Matt's called a widow woman he knows at Quartz City, name of Mrs. Callahan. She owns a couple of boardinghouses. In order not to arouse any more suspicion than possible, we'll split up. Joe, you and Hildy can stay at one of Mrs. Callahan's boardinghouses. Nate, you and Ruby stay at another. Spud and I will stay at a hotel.

"Let's all stay away from each other as much as possible so nobody knows we're together. We'll meet each evening at a little secluded place Matt told me about. It's just outside of town. There we'll compare notes. Then I'll do the follow-up investigation on whatever rumors or bits of information any of you picks up."

Hildy stirred uneasily. She didn't like the idea of being separated from Ruby or Spud. "Uh . . . Brother Ben, couldn't Ruby and I go together? And maybe Spud?"

The old man smiled, looking at her in the rearview mirror. "It's perfectly natural for kids to find each other and pal around together. So, yes, you may, but don't do anything to make it look as though we all know each other—especially the adults."

Hildy sank back with a satisfied sigh.

Ben continued, "We won't have much time. I met Matt Farnham downtown for an early breakfast. He told me that the fire chief expects school will open a week from today. So we've got just four days to solve this case, because none of us will want to work on Sunday."

Ruby's father, Nate Konning, was a tall, slender man who was variously nicknamed Slim, Highpockets, and Beanpole. A one-time saddle-tramp cowboy, later a despised sheepherder, the blond-haired man now was sometimes called *Preacher* because he had recently felt called to the ministry. However, he had no church, so he worked part-time at odd jobs.

So far on the trip he had said nothing, but now he spoke up. "It ain't—isn't—much time," Nate said doubtfully. He was still trying to improve his grammar to match his new calling. He added heartily, "But we'll do our best! And with the Lord's help, that'll be enough. Isn't that right, Joe?"

"I hope so."

Nate added, "This'll give me a chance to witness to some of those brothers in the mine. Since it's dangerous work, maybe some of them will be ready to listen."

Hildy nodded approvingly and started to say something encouraging, but Ben spoke before she could.

"Did any of you three kids know a girl named Gladys Cassell?"

"Yes," Hildy answered. "We all do. She started school yesterday, same as Spud did—a week late."

Ben asked, "Then you didn't get to know her well?"

Hildy leaned forward anxiously. "No, why? Is something wrong?"

Ben took a long, slow breath before answering. "She was riding home with her father in an old Hudson last night when they were in a wreck."

"Oh, no!" Hildy whispered, remembering the sad-faced girl in the woman's dress cut down to fit.

Ben continued, "Because there's no hospital in Lone River, the ambulance had to come from the county seat at Dos Piedras. It was an hour from the time of the accident before the ambulance came and took her and her father to the hospital."

Hildy swallowed hard. "Are they okay?"

"Her father is, but it was too late for the daughter."

Hildy sank back into the seat, suddenly feeling sick.

Ben said, "That's not the first time somebody was lost because Lone River doesn't have a hospital."

Hildy exclaimed with passion, "If we'd had a hospital, she might still be alive!"

Ben nodded. "We're going to have a hospital—that is, if we can find the highgraders who are stealing from Matt's mine."

Hildy ached too much for Gladys to say anything more, but Ruby spoke up. "I don't unnerstand what yo're a-sayin', Brother Ben."

"Didn't you know?" the old ranger asked with surprise. "That's what Matt intended to do with the profits from his mine—build a hospital for Lone River!"

"He was?" Hildy asked, still hurting for the new girl who had suddenly been snatched from life to death.

"It was Matt's plan," Ben replied. "It wasn't exactly a secret, but he hadn't announced it publicly, either."

Hildy realized it was too late for Gladys, but maybe it wouldn't be for someone else. With sudden hot tears blurring her vision, Hildy leaned forward and cried out hoarsely. "Then we're going to catch those highgraders and build that hospital!"

—

CHAPTER FOUR

TROUBLE AT THE BOARDINGHOUSE

Early Wednesday Afternoon

It was nearing noon in the Northern Mines of California's Sierra Nevada foothills when Ben turned the big Packard off the highway onto a dirt side road. He parked under a large valley oak tree, set the handbrake, and turned to face the five other people in the car.

"This is where we split up, folks," he announced. "To avoid suspicion in case the highgraders have someone watching for strangers, Matt Farnham arranged for his mine superintendent to meet us here. His name's Leith Cowan, and he's a pillar in the community who's worked for Matt since he bought the Shasta Daisy Mine.

"Joe, you and Hildy go with Cowan to Mrs. Callahan's Room and Board. Mrs. Callahan is expecting you. Nate, you and Ruby stay with me at the edge of Quartz City. Spud and I will drop you off there. Fortunately, your belongings aren't very heavy, because you'll have to walk a couple of blocks to the Shamrock Rooming House. Mrs. Callahan also owns that.

"She's expecting you, and Matt says you can trust her. But don't tell her or anyone why we're really here. Spud and I will be at the Miner's Hotel, which Mrs. Callahan doesn't own. I would have liked to have a second car meet us, but Matt and I figured it'd be wiser not to let any more people than necessary know who we are and why we're here. Only Cowan knows anything about us, and even he doesn't know why we're here."

The old ranger turned to look out the window as a dusty Dodge sedan bumped up the road toward them. "That must be him now."

Hildy watched Leith Cowan slide out of the car, glance around, then hurry to the Packard. Everyone got out to meet the mine superintendent. He was in his late thirties, of slender build but with a potbelly starting to show. His rounded face, swarthy skin, brown eyes and prominent nose were offset by black hair. It was neatly combed, parted in the middle and showed no hint of gray, not even at the temples.

He was a friendly man with a big smile and a hearty hand-shake, even for Hildy, Ruby, and Spud. When introductions had been made all around, he turned to the old ranger. "When Matt phoned to say you were coming, he didn't say why, but that you'd fill me in."

"Since we're pressed for time, Leith, why don't we do that later?"

"Of course. All right, who's going with me?"

Joe Corrigan said, "My daughter and me. Hildy, you get in Mr. Cowan's car while I get our things out of Ben's trunk."

A short time later, Mr. Cowan turned the dusty Dodge around and turned north onto a narrow but paved road that wound around the tree-covered mountains. He explained, "We'll be in Gold County and Quartz City in fifteen minutes or so. Next to Nevada County and its main cities of Grass Valley and Nevada City, Gold County and Quartz City are the only places in the whole country that aren't feeling the Depression."

Joe Corrigan shifted in the right-front passenger seat to look at the peaceful mountainsides. "I've thought about moving up here permanently, but Hildy wants to stay in Lone River."

"Lots of other people have already moved up here, but they can't get jobs," Cowan said. "In a little while, you'll see thousands of those folks camped in cardboard shanties or old tents, all hoping to get on at the mines.

"I don't have time to read, myself, but I heard these people came here after some national magazine—the *Saturday Evening Post*, I think it was—ran a story about this being the only part of the country where there is plenty of work."

"Guess Nate and I are lucky to get work in the mines," Joe said.

"Mr. Corrigan, I hate to tell you this, but with a name like Corrigan, you can't work in the mines."

Hildy was startled. From the look on her father's face, he was too.

He asked, "Why not?"

"Hardrock miners are almost all Cornishmen. They're considered the best in the world, but they're clannish. They're called 'Cousin Jacks' because they're always saying they have a cousin by that name who wants to work in the mines. So you'll see signs in bars and places when you get to town, saying: 'No Irish.' I'm sorry, Joe, but even in my position, I wouldn't dare put you down in the mines, because it would cause trouble."

Hildy leaned forward in the back seat to ask anxiously, "But he has to get a job there!" She caught a warning look from her father and remembered Ben's caution about telling anyone anything.

Joe Corrigan jumped in quickly. "How about a job above ground, then?"

Cowan shook his head. "Not even there—nowhere around the mines. However, you can probably get on with the railroad. It's all Irish, and they're as clannish as the Cousin Jacks are in the mines."

"What railroad?" Hildy inquired.

"The G.C.Q.C.—stands for Gold County, Quartz City—is a narrow-gauge short line that hauls the gold from the mines to

Colfax. There the Southern Pacific picks it up and takes it to the mint in San Francisco. The G.C.Q.C. agent there owes me a favor, so I'll give him a call. Don't worry! You'll have a job, Joe, although it can't be in any mine."

Hildy slid back in the seat and rode the rest of the way in silence, her mind spinning. The unexpected development because of bigotry would hinder Brother Ben's plans to get two trusted men inside the mine to find out who was stealing the gold. Her uncle Nate's surname of Konning could be of any national origin, she thought, so he'd get to work in the Shasta Daisy.

Hildy decided that having the two fathers in different jobs might work out even better. Maybe the stolen gold was being shipped from the mines by rail, and her father could pick up some clues about that. Hildy could hardly wait to share her conclusion with her father, Ben, and the others.

If Joe Corrigan felt any concern about learning he couldn't work in the Shasta Daisy, he hid it well. He asked Cowan about life in Quartz City.

Cowan replied with enthusiasm, saying that even though Quartz City was a wide-open town where the bars never closed, it was generally peaceful with lots of churches.

Hildy shifted the conversation to the scenery. "Everything's so beautiful!" she exclaimed. "What are those tall trees we're passing?"

Cowan looked out the window and answered. "Those are yellow pines, but locally they're called ponderosas. Mixed in with them you'll see digger pines and black, valley, and live oaks. Those shrubs with small leaves and twisted reddish branches are manzanita. Those other shrubs that have lost their leaves are California buckeye."

Hildy's natural curiosity helped her remember the names and shapes as she felt the Dodge start down a steep hill. She glanced ahead and saw they were heading toward a bridge over a river at the bottom of a canyon.

"Look around," Mr. Cowan instructed, shifting down so the

car wouldn't gain speed going downhill. "For the next five miles or so you'll see the unemployed people I told you about."

The camps were spread out along the riverbank on both sides of the stream. Hildy was used to seeing sharecroppers' cabins, canvas tents, and tarpaper shacks, but it had been a long time since she'd seen so many crude shelters and tired-looking, skinny people. There was such a look of hopelessness on the faces of those she saw sitting idly on the bridge railing.

She felt compassion for them, because she had known hunger and poverty all her life, but she had a hope and a dream that someday she'd leave such things behind. From the looks in these peoples' eyes, she decided they had no such vision. They had given up all but life itself.

"How do they live?" Joe asked as the sedan left the bridge and started climbing out of the canyon on the other side.

"I've heard they steal from nearby ranchers, maybe butcher a stray cow now and then, or they poach deer and an occasional bear—whatever they can find to eat."

Gladys Cassell's thin face came to mind again, and Hildy felt a sense of sadness sweep over her. Yesterday Gladys had the same hungry, tired look in her eyes as these people they had just passed. Now Gladys was gone, her life lost because there was no hospital in Lone River.

Hildy's thoughts were broken by the sound of an airplane flying low overhead. She had seen only a few planes in her life, so she bent her head to look up at the biplane as it climbed sharply into the sky.

Leith Cowan explained, "There's a small airport over to the east. Well, it's more of a dirt landing strip. Hardly ever used." He paused, then added, "Hear the stamp mills? They run day and night, crushing rock for the gold. That tells us we're coming into Quartz City."

The steady thump of the stamps grew louder as Hildy gazed at the city spread out over several hills. Houses were scattered throughout the hills covered with ponderosas. Some Victorian-style homes clung precariously to the steep eastern side of a hill above a small creek. Three church steeples, glistening white as though freshly painted, rose above the trees on the highest hill.

"See that red adobe-brick church through those trees?" Cowan asked. "That's the one I attend. Come hear our choir. Cornishmen are the world's best singers."

"Thanks," Joe Corrigan replied. "Where are the mines?"

"Back up those side canyons." Cowan pointed to the east. "See that derrick-like structure sticking up in the air? That's the headframe on the Shasta Daisy. A headframe is about 90 feet tall and has two purposes. It's used to pull gold ore and tailings or waste from the mine on cars running on rails. Men and equipment are also lowered into the mine from the base of the headframe—"

"Oh, what a cute little train!" Hildy broke in.

"That's the narrow gauge I was telling you about," the driver explained. "You can walk down and take a better look at it after you're settled, because that's your boardinghouse just beyond the tracks."

Mrs. Callahan's Room and Board was an immense, two-story wooden structure barely half a block beyond the railroad tracks. Once it had probably been painted gray, but smoke from the passing train engines had made it a dirty gray-black.

Mrs. Callahan was a big woman with a flushed, red face, immense arms, and a voice like a thunder clap. "Any friend of Matt Farnham is a friend of mine!" she exclaimed, shaking Joe Corrigan's hand vigorously. This caused the loose flesh beneath her upper arm to jiggle. Hildy managed to evade the handshake by backing up a step and hanging on to the cardboard suitcase that held her meager belongings.

After Leith Cowan left, the landlady led Hildy and her father down a long, narrow hallway, past closed doors on both sides. She paused at one marked 9, and inserted a long slender passkey in the hole beneath a white doorknob.

"Two single beds, one in each room," she explained, pulling a string inside the door. An electric light in the center of the room snapped on, the bulb swinging wildly from a long, frayed cord suspended from the ceiling.

Hildy stepped gingerly inside, seeing that it was a simple room but nicer than anything she'd ever had. There was an ancient dresser with a cracked mirror, a rickety table with an enamelware wash pan and pitcher, and one straight-backed chair. Through the two grimy windowpanes, Hildy could see a high concrete sidewalk, a paved street, and the railroad tracks beyond. Through the connecting door, Hildy glimpsed a second bedroom and guessed it was similarly furnished.

Mrs. Callahan explained, "Bath's down the hall to the right. Meals in the parlor at regular hours, and them that comes late usually goes hungry."

Hildy liked Mrs. Callahan, in spite of her brash manner. Hildy's father thanked the landlady, accepted a key for himself and one for Hildy, then closed the outside door. Hildy heard heavy feet clumping down the hallway.

Hildy's father took the second bedroom, so Hildy dropped her suitcase on the bed, which squeaked with the light load. She started to look around for a closet when Mrs. Callahan's voice came through the thin walls.

"Watch your tongue, Casper Cobb, or I'll fix it so you won't never be bothered with it again!"

Hildy smiled, imagining the big woman facing down some miner. Then Hildy's smile faded as a man's voice challenged the landlady.

"Why, you old war horse! I've got half a notion to pitch you out in the street!"

Hildy looked anxiously around as her father hurried through the connecting bedroom door, quickly opened the outside one, and stepped into the hallway.

Hildy followed him. She saw past Mrs. Callahan's broad back to a short, stocky man whose nose had obviously been broken and not healed straight. His long, untidy, graying black hair was thinning, falling over his hard, cold, blue eyes.

Hildy's father asked softly, "Trouble, Mrs. Callahan?"

She didn't look around. "Nothing I can't handle, but thanks

anyway," she said. Then she pointed past the stocky man to the open door behind him. "I told you before, Cas—no smoking in your room. Now, get your things and skedaddle before I lose my temper!"

For a moment, Casper Cobb, whom Hildy judged to be in his mid-fifties, glowered at Joe as though debating whether to take out his anger on the new arrival. Then the man's eyes shifted to Hildy. He blinked and snapped his head back as if he had been hit on the chin.

Hildy watched in surprise as the man studied her, a frown sliding over his face. When Mrs. Callahan spoke sharply to him, he turned wordlessly back into his room.

Hildy and her father returned to their room to finish unpacking. A few minutes later, Hildy looked out the window as Casper Cobb passed beneath it.

Suddenly, Hildy tensed and stared hard. The evicted man wore old cowboy jeans, boots, and a black, flat pancake hat. He set his wicker suitcase down, pulled out "the makin's" and rolled a cigarette with one hand.

"Daddy!" Hildy's voice rose with sharp urgency. "Come here, quick!"

When her father hurried to Hildy's side, the old cowboy was moving down the sidewalk in a rolling gait.

"What's the matter?" Hildy's father asked.

"That man!" Hildy exclaimed, pointing through the window. "I think he's the same one who was driving the car at the bank, the car the tall stranger got into after dropping some stolen gold in Mr. Farnham's office."

"You sure, Hildy?" her father asked doubtfully. "You said you didn't get a good look at the driver."

"I didn't, but I'm sure he's the one, because of that hat. And did you notice the strange way he acted when he saw me in the hallway? I'm sure he recognized me too!"

Hildy turned anxious eyes on her father. "Do you think that means I'm in danger?"

—

CHAPTER FIVE

MORE STRANGE
HAPPENINGS

Wednesday Afternoon

Hildy's father put his strong arm around her narrow shoulders. "I don't think you're in any danger, because I understand miners don't take kindly to men who harm girls. But be careful. Stay close to Ruby or Spud while I'm away. Now, finish unpacking and find your cousin. I'll see Leith Cowan to find out if he managed to get me an appointment with the man at the railroad."

After asking Mrs. Callahan for directions to the Shamrock Rooming House, Hildy started down the street toward the train depot. The heavy thump of the distant stamp mills sounded incessantly over the town.

She was pleased that the little black engine was still there, although the tiny cars had been shunted off to a siding a couple of blocks away.

As Hildy passed the loading platform at the depot, she broke into a big smile. Ruby was just crossing the tracks, coming toward her. Hildy hurried to meet her cousin.

41

"Guess who I saw at the boardinghouse where Daddy and I are staying?" Hildy began. Without waiting for Ruby to reply, Hildy told about Casper Cobb and said she was sure he had recognized her. "Maybe we'd better find Spud and tell him too," she concluded.

"He kin take keer of hisse'f," Ruby said, her tone showing the disregard she held for the freckled-faced boy. "I want to git a closer look at that thar little train engine. It's cuter 'an a bug's ear."

The girls walked along the graveled railroad bed. Hildy was glad she and Ruby were wearing shoes, even though Hildy usually preferred being barefoot.

As they drew near the locomotive, Ruby marveled. "It don't look big enough to haul them other cars. Why, this here engine ain't but about twenty feet long, I bet, not more'n half the size of a reg'lar engine, maybe even only a quarter as big."

A man's voice said, "That's because it's a narrow gauge, girls. And don't let its size fool you. That's a powerful little steam locomotive."

Startled, Hildy whirled around. A clean-shaven old man, slender as a lead pencil, sat whittling against the side of the loading platform by the depot. The traditional railroader's striped overalls seemed much too big for his frail body. He wore the matching railroader's cap. A scratched lunch pail was on the ground between his rough work shoes. His little toe stuck out of the right shoe.

"What's narrow gauge mean?" Hildy asked, deciding this elderly man was safe to talk to, although she'd been taught all her life not to speak to strangers.

"Rails are measured by the distance between the inner edges or heads," he explained, folding up his jackknife and slipping it into his right front pocket. With his left hand, he took the sharpened end of the kitchen match he'd been whittling and popped it into the corner of his mouth. "Standard gauge is normally four feet, eight-and-a-half inches. Narrow gauge is three feet or less."

Hildy wanted to know more, but Ruby tugged gently on the

back of Hildy's dress where the old man couldn't see.

"Let's get closer to that ol' engine," Ruby whispered.

Hildy nodded to Ruby and said to the old railroader, "Thanks, mister." She instinctively liked him.

"Call me Skeezix," he replied. "I worked this line forty years, then they made me re-tire. Ain't got kith nor kin, and nothin' to do all day, so I still come down here and watch the trains go by. But nobody wants an ol' man around, 'cepting sometimes kids."

Hildy felt compassion for the man. "We have to go," she said, "but maybe sometime we can stay longer."

As the cousins turned west toward the business section of town, Skeezix called after them. "Hope you'll come back soon, 'cause they're going to make up the gold train."

Hildy and Ruby looked at each other, then looked back at the railroader. "Gold train?" Hildy asked.

The man's deeply lined face broke into a grin. His hazel eyes shone with pleasure. "Thought that'd get your attention, gals! Yessiree, when the mines have melted the gold down into bars called ingots, they're sneaked onto this short line to Colfax, where the gold's transferred to the regular railroad for shipment to the mint in San Francisco."

Hildy frowned thoughtfully. "I'd think the mine owners and the railroad people would keep that a secret so nobody'd try to rob the gold train."

Skeezix chuckled and slapped his open palm against his right knee. "Oh, they try! They try hard! I mean, they try to keep it secret, and they do from most people. And so far, nobody's ever tried to rob the train.

"As for knowing when it's happening, well, when a man sits as long as I have, just watching trains, it's no trick to figure out when the gold's going to be shipped. You see, people being creatures of habit, they always make up a gold train different from other trains, yet exactly the same way each time the ingots are going to be aboard. You got time, I'll tell you about it."

Hildy and Ruby exchanged glances, then Hildy remembered

that she wanted to find Spud and tell him about recognizing the driver of the Model A. "We'd love to, Mr. Skeezix," she said, "but we can't."

"Skeezix," he replied as the girls started off again. "Just plain Skeezix."

The cousins discussed the exciting discovery that there was going to be a gold shipment. That might mean the highgraders would have their gold on board too. But how could they do that? If they managed to get their stolen gold on the train, how was it switched from heading for the mint in San Francisco to end up in Mexico?

Ruby moaned, "Ain't no way we're a-gonna figger this thing out afore our time runs out and we gotta git back to Lone River!"

Hildy shook her head. "We have to try. Anyway, it's all very challenging. Oh, look! There's the Miner's Hotel, where Spud and Brother Ben are staying."

The cousins debated the wisdom of going directly to the long, narrow, one-story frame building tucked in between old red adobe-brick structures with iron shutters now used as shops.

Even though she was eager for Spud to know about seeing the driver of the Model A and the possible tie-in with the gold train, Hildy decided against going to the hotel.

"In case somebody's watching us—like that Casper Cobb or even the stranger Spud and I followed—we'd better not go in. We could hang around, hoping Spud or Brother Ben will come out, but that might look suspicious. I don't think it will hurt anything to wait until we have our meeting tonight outside of town."

Ruby shrugged. "Suits me. Then how about us a-pokin' around town to see if'n we kin meet some kids an' maybe learn somethin' from them? Daddies sometimes talk careless-like in front of their chillun, ye know."

Hildy agreed. They stopped the first man they saw and asked where the school was. They followed the directions, crossing the tracks again and heading east along a narrow, paved road. It led into a canyon lined with ponderosa and digger pines. The ground-shaking thump of the stamp mills grew louder.

Hildy and Ruby located the school with its bell tower, but the building was silent. There weren't even any kids in the rocky, irregular school yard. Disappointed, the cousins started to turn back toward town when Hildy spotted a towering wooden structure.

"I think that's what Mr. Cowan called a headframe. Let's go take a look."

The girls started up the narrow, winding road toward the structure that marked the entrance to a mine. Along the way, they saw a boy about their age walking near some crushed rocks and other debris off to the right side of the road, not far from the headframe.

Hildy saw that he wore heavy shoes, dark pants, and a blue shirt with sleeves rolled up above the elbows. His eyes were on the ground. He frequently bent to pick up something that he dropped into a round tin container with a narrow neck and tight-fitting lid.

Ruby asked, "What's he a-doin'? Pickin' up rocks?"

"Looks that way. I'd guess this big pile of stones and things came from the mine. But let's find out."

Hildy and Ruby left the road and carefully eased through strands of barbed wire. They started walking over the acres of debris toward the boy. His back was to them, and he seemed unaware of their approach.

Hildy opened her mouth to call a greeting, but tensed at the distinctive sound of a Model A Ford on the roadway. She looked back and stopped dead still. "That looks like the same car Spud and I saw in Lone River!" she exclaimed.

"Ain't hardly likely. Come on, let's go talk to that thar boy."

Hildy hesitated, knowing that Ruby was probably right. Still, Hildy couldn't help staring at the vehicle as it moved along the road heading toward town. She could see that there were two men inside. The driver looked tall enough to be the man she and Spud had followed from the bank in Lone River. Hildy couldn't see the passenger.

"Come on!" Ruby cried impatiently. "That boy's gittin' farther and farther away!"

Hildy started to obey just as the driver of the Model A looked out of his open window toward her. She saw him do a double take. His mouth moved, and he said something to the other man. The car swerved to the shoulder and stopped. The driver stuck his head out the window so the afternoon sun shone clearly on his face.

Hildy whispered, "It's him! I'm sure it's him!"

"Then let's git outta here!" Ruby picked up her skirt to raise it above her knees so she could run easier.

Hildy did the same, turning away just as the stranger leaped from the car. "Hey!" he yelled, running across the road toward the barbed-wire fence. "Hey, wait!"

The girls didn't wait. They broke into a run across the rough, uneven ground toward the boy. He turned toward the girls as the stranger shouted again.

Running up to the boy, Hildy explained, "That man's after us!" She looked back and pointed.

The second man had also gotten out of the car but stood on the running board, looking over the top of the Model A. He was a stranger.

Hildy whirled back to the boy. "He'll hurt us! Where can we hide?"

The boy hesitated a moment, then pointed. "See that little hill over there? When you get to the other side, he can't see you. Turn left. There's an old mine shaft hidden behind manzanita. Duck just inside the entrance and stay quiet. I'll send him off in the other direction!"

"Thanks!" Hildy cried, glancing back. The passenger still stood on the running board, but the driver was trying to get through the fence. He was having trouble because he had snagged the seat of his pants on the top strand of wire. He was twisted at an awkward angle, making it harder to free himself.

"Don't jist stand thar a-lookin'!" Ruby chided, stopping a few feet ahead. "Let's run!"

Hildy nodded and ran after her cousin. They topped a high mound of broken rock and dropped down on the other side. The boy had been right. The man couldn't see the cousins now. The girls turned sharply left and raced toward the dense reddish manzanita at the end of the dump.

They found a small opening in the ten-foot tall undergrowth and plunged through. Ruby panted, "Shore hope we don't run into no b'ar in here!"

"Don't think about it! Just keep moving!"

The girls emerged on the other side of the manzanita to find themselves at the foot of a small mountain. Hildy had never seen a mine shaft before, but when she saw an opening in the side of the hill, she was sure what it was.

She led the way to the aging timbers that formed an inverted U at the opening. She swallowed hard, fighting the claustrophobia that made her afraid of narrow, enclosed places. She was reluctant to enter the dark place, but decided there was no other choice. She hesitated, trying to see into the gloomy interior, then entered cautiously.

Hildy and Ruby were still catching their breath when they saw the man who was after them standing on the hill where they had dropped out of his sight. He stood there for about a minute, then turned away. The girls sighed with relief.

About fifteen minutes later they were debating whether it was safe to leave when the boy with the bucket appeared on top of the hill. "They're gone," he called through cupped hands. "You can come out now."

Hildy and Ruby met the boy at the top of the hill. He asked, "Why'd Trey chase you?"

"You know him?" Hildy asked.

"Sure! Trey Granger worked in the Shasta Daisy where my dad was shift boss."

"Shasta Daisy?" Hildy echoed.

"Uh-huh. So did that other fellow with him. His name's Garrett Kayne. But Trey wouldn't tell me why he was after you girls, so how about you telling me?"

Hildy exchanged glances with her cousin, then introduced herself and Ruby.

"I'm Jack Tremayne," the boy replied.

Hildy didn't want to tell anyone about the reason Trey Granger had chased them, but she couldn't think how to avoid answering. So she hedged. "It's a long story." Quickly she changed the subject. "What are you doing?"

"Picking up gold-bearing quartz and putting it in my Cousin Jack lunch pail." He removed the lid and lifted out half a dozen pieces of what looked like plain rock. Jack explained, "Quartz rock has gold in it. Most of it's recovered at the stamp mills you hear. An ore car from the mine comes out here on those little rails you can see in the distance and dumps the waste rock from the mine. Sometimes us kids come out here after school and try to find ore-bearing quartz, like this." He hoisted the bucket slightly.

Ruby asked, "Whatcha gonna do with it?"

"I smash the quartz and sell the gold for enough to help feed my mother and kid sisters and brothers."

Hildy frowned. "I thought you said your father worked in the mine."

"Did. He got killed a couple months ago. He was back in the mine when some unstable dynamite must've gotten jarred or shook. Anyway, it blew up."

Hildy whispered, "I'm sorry!"

The boy nodded, and Hildy noticed his blue eyes had suddenly become misty. "That man who stood at the car—Garrett Kayne—was the last person to see Dad alive. Now he's got Dad's old job as shift boss."

Jack's voice rose. "What makes me mad is that Dad had fired Kayne only a couple days before. The night he was fired, he came up to Dad on the street and started a fist fight. Now—" the boy's voice trailed off.

Hildy instinctively reached out and touched the boy's arm in a gesture of sympathy just as a shadow fell across the area. Hildy glanced up. The sun was starting to slide down behind the ponderosas on the western slope. Hildy remembered that it was time to head for the meeting with Brother Ben and the others.

She quickly said goodbye and left with Ruby. As they eased through the fence, Hildy lowered her voice. "I'd like to talk to Jack again. Maybe he can help us solve this case."

"I was jist a-thinkin' the same thing."

"He must go to this school, so maybe we can see him there tomorrow. Anyway, we'll sure have a lot to share at our meeting tonight."

"Shore will! But I been a-thinkin'. Now that them two men you'n Spud follered in Lone River—Casper Cobb an' Trey Granger—know yo're here, ye kin bet yore bottom dollar they're not a-gonna like it one little bit! The question is, what'll they *do* about it? An' *when*?"

CHAPTER SIX

STRANGERS IN THE NIGHT

Wednesday Evening and Night

Night had barely settled over the foothills when the six investigators drifted in by twos to a secluded stand of ponderosas and incense cedars just outside of Quartz City. The thudding of the distant stamp mills was muted but steady, like a heartbeat that never ceased, day or night.

Brother Ben, the former lawman, asked each person in turn to report on the day's events. Hildy and Ruby, eager to share their experiences, spoke first.

They told about Skeezix and the gold train, being chased by Trey Granger while Garrett Kayne watched, and how Jack Tremayne had saved them.

When they had finished, the old ranger said, "There's no doubt you girls are in some danger. Joe and Nate, would you like me to take them back to Lone River where they'd be safer?"

Both girls instantly protested so loudly that their fathers reluctantly agreed they could stay in Quartz City.

Ruby's father reported on his day's activities. "The mine superintendent said Matt Farnham had told him on the phone to give me a job that would let me roam freely through the mines, although the banker didn't say why and Leith Cowan didn't ask me. He named some possibilities: specimen boss, carpenter, electrician, mule skinner, and tool nipper."

"What are those last two?" Hildy asked.

"Lots of mules are used in the mines, so somebody has to drive them. I could do that, but tool nipper suits me better. That means I pick up tools in need of repair, or deliver them, along with other supplies, like explosives. I start tomorrow if I can buy or borrow some miners' clothes and boots."

Ruby's father added that he had heard some muckers coming out of the mines mention the death of their former shift boss, John Tremayne. Muckers were the men who used hands or machines to load broken rock onto cars in the mine. They wondered how such an experienced hardrock miner would have been careless enough around "sweating" dynamite to have set it off.

Hildy asked, "What's 'sweating' dynamite?"

Her uncle explained. "As I understand it, sometimes a box or even a stick of dynamite gets old, like when it's forgotten and left a long time in one place. The nitroglycerin—that's an explosive liquid—then seeps out. It shows up on the outside of the dynamite stick as little pale yellow or amber droplets, like sweat on a man's brow.

"Usually, dynamite is safe as long as the detonating cap or fuse isn't set off. But when the dynamite 'sweats,' the nitro is so unstable that it can be accidentally set off by bumping or jarring it. That's apparently what happened to John Tremayne, although he was alone at the time, so nobody knows for sure."

Hildy shuddered, thinking about the dangers in mining, and wishing her uncle wasn't working a mile underground. She was grateful that her father hadn't been able to get a job at the Shasta Daisy.

Joe Corrigan began his report by mentioning the incident at Mrs. Callahan's Room and Board where she'd evicted Casper Cobb. "When I asked Mrs. Callahan if she was having trouble,"

Joe added, "I thought Cobb was going to take me on too."

Hildy smiled in the darkness. "I think he backed down when he saw how strong-looking you are, Daddy."

"Maybe so, but he's a rough character. It's obvious from his crooked nose and cauliflower ears that he's been a boxer or wrestler. My guess is that he backed down because I'm about twenty years younger. Anyway, Hildy later saw him outside her window and told me she's quite sure he was driving the car she and Spud followed in Lone River."

After discussion of what danger that might pose for Hildy or Spud, Joe finished his report. There hadn't been an opening at the railroad station, not even for someone with an Irish name like Corrigan. But Leith Cowan's friend at the depot had created one. "They started me right away—as the janitor. It gives me a chance to move around the whole depot and try to hear things."

Next Spud reported on his investigation. "Not much happened," he began. "I poked around town but didn't see or hear anything of interest—that is, until I returned to the Miner's Hotel, where Brother Ben and I are staying."

"What happened?" Hildy asked.

"I saw this man Casper Cobb leaving. Apparently he'd wanted a room, but there wasn't any."

Ben Strong said, "I'm sure you're right, Spud. In fact, Nevada County and Gold County are probably the only two places in the nation where you can't get a room without a reservation. Good thing Matt Farnham had connections and could get us lodgings."

Hildy asked, "Did that man—Mr. Cobb—see you, Spud?"

"No, I don't think so. And I didn't recognize him, maybe because he was too far away. But he was wearing the clothes you described, so I'm sure he's the same man."

Discussion followed on who that man might be. Then the meeting drifted off into generalities. Brother Ben ended the session by assigning everyone specific things to do before meeting back at the same spot the following night: "Joe, please see what you can learn about the gold train.

"Nate, please try to find out about Cobb, Granger, and Kayne, who work in the mine, especially about the fight Kayne had with John Tremayne after he fired Kayne.

"Spud, I'd like you to get acquainted with some kids from the local school. Try to get them to talk about highgrading, because kids overhear things adults say. If you have time, and they'll let you on the grounds, try to look around the Shasta Daisy. Probably nobody'd suspect your motives, because of your age.

"Hildy, will you and Ruby follow up on that boy, Jack? Get details of what happened to his father and what he knows about Granger, Kayne, and maybe Cobb.

"It would help if all of us tried to learn something about hardrock mining. But above all, be careful. Hildy, I'm concerned because the two men you and Spud saw in Lone River realize you're here. They're bound to wonder why, and they'll surely guess there's a tie-in with the bank.

"Maybe you and Spud shouldn't be seen together, because if those men saw you, they'd know for sure something was up, and that you wouldn't be up here without some adults. The one good thing is that we now know the names of those men. I'll check them out with my law-enforcement contacts here and see what I can learn.

"Time's running out fast, but we made progress today, and we've still got three days to solve this case. So, be careful, and we'll see each other here tomorrow night."

That night Hildy lay awake, listening to the incessant thumping of the stamp mills and the throbbing of a town that never slept. She had closed the windows against the brisk October air, but she still heard faint music and laughter, along with her father's snoring. It was so loud that even the door between their rooms couldn't shut out the sound. Occasionally, the short-line locomotive rattled by on the nearby tracks.

In spite of the sounds, Hildy's mind was active with the excitement and challenge of trying to solve the mystery of the phantom gold by Saturday night.

At last she got up, thinking that since she couldn't sleep, she'd read her Bible awhile. As she stood in the darkened room, she glanced out the window just as a cream-colored Model A coupe climbed the steep main street.

Hildy ran to the window in her homemade nightgown. Her thick brunette hair, loosened from the daytime braids, cascaded over her face. She brushed it back to better watch the car. It parked near a streetlight, where the driver stepped out and onto the concrete sidewalk.

"It's Trey Granger!" Hildy whispered to herself. "And he's carrying something." She pressed her forehead against the cold pane to see better.

She noticed the tall man was carrying a canvas bag about eight inches tall and six inches wide at the bottom. The top was tied with a drawstring.

Impulsively, Hildy decided to follow him. She hurriedly pulled her dress on over the ankle-length nightgown. It showed several inches below her dress, but it was night and she figured nobody would notice. She slid bare feet into her shoes but didn't stop to tie them. All the while she stayed in the darkness of the room but close to the window, so she could keep an eye on Trey Granger. Grabbing her key and a sweater, Hildy tiptoed out of her room, down the empty hallway, and out the front door. She was just in time to see Granger turn a corner about a block up the street.

She started running after him while struggling to get into her sweater, hoping she'd be able to find Trey when she got to the corner. The long nightgown beneath her dress bound her legs, so Hildy glanced around, didn't see anyone, and pulled both garments above her knees. This allowed her to run faster, but the steep street soon had her puffing.

She passed cars with their wheels turned against the curb to prevent runaways. The streetlights were bright enough to keep Hildy from being afraid. A slight, brisk wind rattled the slender Chinese trees of heaven that grew everywhere, even in the small patch of dirt between the sidewalk and some stores, now silent with great iron shutters across them.

Panting and feeling a stitch develop in her side, Hildy drew near the street where she'd seen Trey Granger disappear. About two-thirds of the way up the street the businesses had given way to old residences. Hildy slowed, trying to control her breathing so she could hear Granger's footsteps. Hearing none, she gingerly poked her head around the pyracantha hedge surrounding a quaint old Victorian home.

There! she thought, seeing a shadow from a distant streetlight. She withdrew her head and pressed as close as she dared to the pyracantha's sharp thorns. By holding her breath and straining hard to hear, she made out the sound of footsteps. *But are they going away or coming in this direction?*

Carefully, Hildy sneaked another look. *He's coming back— without the sack. I've got to get out of here before he sees me!*

She glanced around for somewhere to hide. The closest place was inside the yard beyond the pyracantha hedge. She took a couple of quick steps and tried to open the iron gate, but it was locked. She started to climb over, but the ancient rusted hinges squeaked so loudly Hildy immediately abandoned the idea. There was nothing left to do but run back the way she'd come.

It was easier going downhill, but her new shoes, with untied laces, kept slipping and threatening to fly off with each running step, and the leather soles sounded like a giant's seven-league boots clumping along. Fearfully, she stole a glance backward just as she passed under a streetlight.

Trey Granger had rounded the corner by the pyracantha. "Hey!" he called, starting to run toward Hildy. "Wait up!"

The girl whirled like a frightened doe and dashed down the street toward the railroad tracks and the safety of her boarding-house.

Hildy was fast, but the man was faster. Even without looking back, she could hear he was rapidly gaining on her. Desperately she looked around for some way of escape.

Her probing eyes found doorways to shuttered businesses, but these were traps with no way out.

Frantically, Hildy turned her eyes back to the railroad tracks and the boardinghouse beyond. They were now closer. *Maybe,* she told herself as her frightened, ragged breathing made noises in the night, *maybe I can just get there! Or get close enough to yell for Daddy!*

Her pursuer had run wordlessly after his first call to wait, but suddenly he called out again—but not to Hildy. "Cas, it's the girl! Stop her!"

Hildy didn't hear the name, and she didn't understand to whom Trey had called because there was nobody on the street. Then a car door opened and a man leaped out. *Casper Cobb!*

He ran from the car, leaped up on the high curb and set himself, legs braced, to stop her.

Lord, what now? It was a silent prayer, a cry for help. Caught between the two men, she had no choice but to turn away. She spotted an opening between two adobe buildings and plunged into it. She stumbled over something soft. A frightened cat let out a screech and fled down the narrow passageway, invisible but making such a racket that the girl could follow its flight.

Hildy reached the other end, slowed by some Chinese trees of heaven that partially blocked her path, then broke into the opening onto another street. Instinctively, she turned east again, hoping to get across the tracks and back to the boardinghouse.

She reached the corner, feeling relieved that the narrow passage between the buildings had apparently slowed her pursuer. But as she sprinted across the intersection, a shadow erupted from deeper shadows. The streetlight gave enough light so that she recognized Cas Cobb. He was within fifty feet, running as fast as his short bow legs would allow.

Oh, no! Hildy moaned, fighting for breath and fearful for her safety. She forced herself to keep running toward the railroad tracks, which were now just a few feet away.

As she neared the first graveled spur of narrow-gauge tracks, her untied right shoe slipped halfway off. Hildy staggered and started to fall. She instinctively reached out her right hand to the only available support—the end of a railroad car.

Balancing on one foot in the shadows and trying to get the shoe back on, Hildy risked looking back. By the streetlight, she saw that Trey Granger had squeezed through the narrow opening between the buildings. He ran toward her, side by side with Cas Cobb, and gaining fast.

Sucking in ragged gulps of air, Hildy groaned with despair. Suddenly she felt fingers close from behind on her right arm. She instinctively tried to jerk away, but the grip was too tight.

She started to scream just as a rough hand clamped across her mouth.

CHAPTER SEVEN

―

A SHOCKING REMARK

Wednesday Night and Thursday Morning

Hildy dropped her shoe and grabbed with both hands at the hand clamped across her mouth. She yanked hard but uselessly against the strong fingers. Double panic swept over her, because she was caught and because she felt she would suffocate. She'd been running hard and gulping air through her open mouth. Now she couldn't get enough air. She tried crying out, but made only muffled sounds.

"Shh!" a man's voice whispered in Hildy's ear. She felt his whiskery face against her cheek. From the darkness, the voice added, "It's me—Skeezix! Be quiet! I'm going to help you."

Hardly daring to believe the words, Hildy relaxed slightly, but not much because she could hear her pursuers drawing closer at a dead run.

The retired railroader whispered again: "I'm going to take my hand off your mouth. Then you crouch down and don't make a sound. I'll get rid of those men."

Numbly, Hildy obeyed. She almost collapsed with relief and weariness in the deep shadows of the boxcar. Skeezix stepped into the glow of the distant streetlight.

The two pursuers puffed to a stop in front of him. Trey asked, "Did you see a girl running this way?"

Before Skeezix could answer, Casper Cobb reached down and picked up Hildy's dropped shoe. "This must be hers!" He turned to face Skeezix. "Which way was she running?"

Skeezix pointed to the right. "She was running in that direction, toward the main line."

"Thanks." Cobb dropped the shoe. "Come on, Trey! She can't get far on this gravel with only one shoe!"

Hildy watched her pursuers run off into the night and disappear behind a string of gondolas and boxcars.

She stood up when the old railroader walked back to her and pressed the shoe into her hand.

He apologized, "Sorry to scare you like I did," he said, "but I was afraid if I didn't put my hand over your mouth, you'd scream, and they'd know where you were."

"It's okay," Hildy said, leaning against the boxcar to slip the shoe on. "Thanks! Thanks a million, Skeezix!"

He chuckled. "I don't hold with telling lies, so when he asked me which way you were running, I told him the truth." He paused, then asked, "Why were they chasing you?"

Hildy bent over and quickly tied both shoes. "I have to get back in case those men return, but if you'll be at the depot tomorrow, I'll come by and tell you."

"Makes sense to me, young lady. See you tomorrow."

Hildy's father was still snoring loudly in the next room when she returned to the boardinghouse. She pulled off her dress and slipped into bed, intending to tell him in the morning what she had done. However, when she awakened, he had already gone to work.

Mrs. Callahan gently chided Hildy for being late to breakfast, but said she'd kept some biscuits and gravy on the back of the stove. Hildy ate quickly and rushed off to meet Ruby.

Hildy told her cousin about the night's experiences, then both hurried to the depot to see Skeezix. Hildy sat next to him on the empty platform and again thanked him for saving her last night.

He smiled. "I live right close and was just out walking when I saw those men chasing you."

Hildy told the old railroader what had happened.

When she finished, Skeezix said, "I'll bet he had gold-bearing quartz in that sack."

Hildy liked the old railroader, but she was a little dubious. Maybe he imagined things. "What makes you think that?" she challenged.

"I know, because people sometimes forget that I'm around, or maybe they just think I'm like some of the other bums that hang around trains. Anyway, they say things, and I listen. Got nothing else to do."

Ruby asked, "What'd ye hear that makes ye think it was a sack o' gold?"

"You can buy sacks like that around here easy, because they're used for carrying gold-bearing ore. And I heard that somebody's being paid off for letting them highgrade from some of the mines. Don't know which mines. There's at least a dozen within twenty miles of here, and you can bet every single one's got somebody stealing from it."

Hildy frowned. "If there was gold in that sack I saw, what happened to it?"

"Granger probably handed it to somebody, or maybe he left it someplace," Skeezix guessed.

"I didn't see or hear anybody else."

The old railroader smiled. "I heard rumors that there's an old white two-story Victorian house on Hardluck Hill Street where a couple times a week sacks like those have been seen on the porch. From what you said, that might be the same street."

"I didn't see a street sign," Hildy admitted.

"Who'd do such a fool thing as leave gold where it kin be stole?" Ruby blurted.

The old man's eyes narrowed thoughtfully. "My guess is that highgraders are leaving a share of their stolen gold for whoever lives in that house. You know, a payoff for being allowed to steal from a mine."

"But what's to stop other folks from swipin' them sacks that are left on the porch?" Ruby asked.

"They're afraid of what will happen to them if the man in that house finds out who robbed him. There's a local saying: 'Highgrading means silence—or death.' I read once that a state official estimates about forty-five percent of all gold is being highgraded from the mines. Fear of being murdered keeps most mouths shut."

"Murdered?" Hildy asked, wondering if she and the rest of the Lone River visitors were in such peril.

"Sure thing! The local newspapers carry stories about murders. They're usually unsolved, but everybody knows it has to be over stolen gold."

Skeezix paused, then added, "Most of the time nobody gets hurt because highgrading is done in secret. But once in a while, somebody does highjack stolen gold. Like the Quartz Hill store owner I heard about who was also a fence for stolen gold. A fence is someone who receives and disposes of stolen gold.

"This Quartz Hill store owner had a quarter million dollars worth in the back room of his store when some guys busted in with shotguns and robbed him. Poor fellow couldn't even report it to the police, because what he was doing was as illegal as what the robbers did." Skeezix slapped his leg in glee.

"Who lives in that white house you mentioned?"

Skeezix shrugged. "Don't know, Hildy. Used to be the Trevor place, but I heard it was recently sold. I don't remember who bought it. Sometimes I forget things."

Hildy asked, "What's the address?"

"Don't know, but it's easy to find. There's an iron fence around it and two big red maples by the gate."

Hildy looked at her cousin. "Let's go see if we can find it."

"You gals be careful!" the old railroader warned.

The cousins climbed Hardluck Hill and easily found the white house. They casually walked by on the opposite side of the street, looking for the occupant's name on a mailbox, but there was none.

Ruby mused, "Reckon we'uns could go ask one of the neighbors."

Hildy shook her head, making the long braids flounce about. "We can't do that, because we don't want to make anyone suspicious. We'll have to watch there tonight."

"Yeah, reckon yo're right. Anyway, it's time to do part of what Brother Ben asked us—see what we kin l'arn about hardrock minin'. But how're we a-gonna do that?"

"How about asking Mr. Cowan? Maybe he'll give us a tour of the Shasta Daisy."

When the girls arrived at the main office, Leith Cowan, the mine superintendent, hastened around his cluttered desk to greet them with a broad smile. "I'm absolutely delighted to see you both!" he exclaimed heartily. "I was hoping we'd have an opportunity to get to know each other better."

"We'd like to know more about mining," Hildy said.

"Come on, I'll give you a tour," Cowan replied, reaching for the doorknob. "I suppose you're both familiar with California history and the Gold Rush?"

"We don't know much about it," Hildy admitted. "We both moved here from out of state this summer."

"Then I'll give you a quick overview as we walk," Cowan said. He led the girls toward the headframe marking the mine shaft opening, explaining that the first gold miners of 1849 found placer, or free gold. This was surface gold that was still found in foothill streams. Early methods included a pan in water to separate gold from dirt and gravel. Panning was still in use by individuals.

Later, miners used hydraulic mining for placer gold. This system used forced powerful streams of water like gigantic garden hoses that washed away whole mountainsides. However, the debris crept into the streams and plugged them with silt. This caused flooding in the valleys below and made those people angry. So the legislature outlawed hydraulic mining.

"So, for some time now," the superintendent concluded, "we've had hardrock mining, or gold-in-place. That's what we're doing here at the Shasta Daisy. The ground we're standing on is riddled with underground shafts or levels, what you might call passageways. They're not tunnels, because they don't open to the surface. All those levels branch off from the shaft, or mine opening. That's where you see the headframe. Down below, the miners blast with powder and then dig for gold, following the vein."

He raised his hand and pointed. "In Nevada County, next to us, there are more than 350 miles of shafts under the county seat. All mines would fill with water if pumps weren't kept working all the—"

"Oh, lookee thar! What're them men a-doin' with that pore old mule?" Ruby interrupted.

Hildy followed in the direction her cousin pointed. A mule had been trussed up in a kind of sling so that only the animal's head and hooves showed.

"Don't worry. That mule's not going to be hurt," Cowan reassured the girls. "They're just getting him ready to lower into the mine to pull ore cars."

Hildy said softly, "He looks so miserable!"

"He'll be fine. Mules in the mines are treated with great respect. Nobody hurts them, and they live a good life underground. They come out only if they start to go blind from being in the darkness so much. Then they're brought back to the surface."

"Don't ye have no 'lectric lights in the mines?" Ruby asked.

"We do now, but miners still need carbide lamps on their hats. In the early days, miners used candles."

The tour took the girls past great stacks of timber. These were used to shore up the underground passages, Cowan explained.

As they moved on, Hildy asked, "What's the biggest vein you've ever found?"

"Most gold is in the quartz rock, so it has to be crushed to remove the ore." Cowan paused, his eyes taking on a strange look Hildy had never seen before.

He continued in a soft, awed tone, "But in this very mine we hit a solid wall of gold as big as the wall in my office."

Ruby made a startled exclamation, but Hildy frowned, still watching their guide's eyes.

For several seconds, he stood in silence. Then he shook his head as if to clear his thoughts. Hildy saw the look vanish from his eyes.

He smiled down at the cousins. "Well, let's continue our tour, shall we?"

"What's all that stuff yonder?" Ruby asked, pointing to a wasteland where a small iron car pulled by a mule was dumping a load of rocks.

Hildy recognized it as the place where they'd met Jack-Tremayne.

Cowan explained, "That's a dump. That little iron car on tracks is taking waste rock up from the underground to be dumped. It's one of the necessary but unprofitable steps in hard-rock mining."

The next-to-last stop on the tour included the refinery, where huge furnaces separated the gold from all that remained. Pure, molten ore was poured into molds. When cooled, the result was gold bars called ingots.

"Finally," Cowan concluded, "these are weighed, tested, and stored until there's enough for a rail shipment to the mint in San Francisco."

Ruby asked, "When's that?"

Their guide smiled but shook his head. "Sorry, but that's a secret." He led the way to his office. "It's nice that you girls could accompany your fathers up from Lone River, but shouldn't you be in school?"

Hildy hesitated before answering, remembering Mr. Farnham's and Brother Ben's warning to be careful about their mission. "There was a gas leak in our school furnace, so classes are suspended for a few days," she explained.

The mine superintendent nodded. "I see." He hesitated, then added, "When Matt Farnham called me to ask if I'd help your fathers get jobs up here, he sounded a little mysterious."

Hildy glanced at Ruby, wondering what to say.

Ruby said, "Ain't all bankers kinda like that? I mean, keepin' things to theirselves?"

Hildy watched Cowan, whose eyelids had drooped slightly, giving him a kind of sleepy but thoughtful look. "I suppose so," he admitted.

"Well," Hildy said cheerfully, "Ruby and I have to go. Thanks for showing us around."

The girls wandered around Quartz Hill, looking in shop windows, and talking about the tour and who might live in the white house on Hardluck Hill. The girls had completed one part of Brother Ben's assignment. They had one more: to learn more about Jack Tremayne.

The cousins were waiting for the boy when school let out that afternoon. He hurried toward them carrying his Cousin Jack lunch pail.

"I'm glad you came," he said with a smile. "Want to go with me while I try to find some gold-bearing quartz?"

Hildy and Ruby readily agreed and fell into step with the miner's son.

Hildy asked, "Does anybody mind your picking up rock that might have gold in it?"

"Naw!" Jack scoffed. "What little there is has been dumped by the mine, so it's like trash. Lots of us kids go out there sometimes and try to find enough to help out our families. In my case, I do it every day because we need the money—my mother and us kids, I mean."

He fell silent, so Hildy and Ruby did the same for a while.

Finally Hildy said, "You're awfully quiet."

Jack stopped and looked at her with sad eyes before answering. Then he spoke in a somber tone. "I've been thinking about something you two might like to know, because maybe the same thing could happen to you."

"What's that?" Hildy asked.

Jack stopped, looked around to be sure nobody was nearby, then lowered his voice and whispered huskily, "I don't think it was an accident that killed my father!"

CHAPTER EIGHT

—

A TERRIBLE SURPRISE

Thursday Afternoon and Evening

Hildy drew back in bewilderment. "Not an accident? I don't understand."

"Me, neither," Ruby added.

The boy looked around again and lowered his voice. "I think it was done on purpose."

Hildy's eyes opened wide in total shock. "But, that would be—" She couldn't say the terrible word.

Jack nodded and answered firmly, "I'm sure somebody caused that unstable dynamite to go off and bury my father under tons of rock."

Hildy shook her head, sending the braids flying. "Oh, you must be mistaken!"

"No, I'm not!" Jack's voice rose. "My father worked in the mines since he was a boy. He knew that bad dynamite was back there, because he told my mother and me. He'd told the powder monkey, the person in charge of explosives around the mine, to get rid of it safely, but before he could, Dad went back there and—" Jack's voice cracked and trailed off.

Hildy and Ruby exchanged stunned glances. Hildy's mind

jumped back to what Jack had said moments before: "It could happen to you." She shuddered, still not wanting to believe Jack, yet fearful he might be telling the truth.

He added quietly, "Dad was too good a hardrock miner to go around that sweating dynamite again, so somebody must have tricked him into going back there alone. When Dad did, someone jarred the powder, making it blow up."

Hildy frowned. "But why would anybody want to do such an awful thing?"

"I don't know. Maybe it had something to do with Dad firing Garrett Kayne. Later, Kayne jumped Dad and they had a big fight. Maybe Dad was on to something and somebody wanted him stopped before he could tell. I don't know who's behind it or why. All I'm sure of is that it was no accident. I'd like to find out who's guilty." Jack sighed. "Maybe if Dad had listened to the tommyknockers, he'd still be here."

"Tommyknockers?" Hildy asked.

"Uh-huh. They're friendly little people who live in the mines and knock to warn miners of danger."

Ruby scoffed, "Don't ye go a-tryin' to josh us!"

"I'm serious," Jack assured her. "Ask any Cornishman who's ever worked the mines about tommyknockers."

Hildy asked thoughtfully, "You mean they're sort of like fairies, elves, or leprechauns?"

Jack smiled. "Everybody knows there's no such things as elves or fairies. But tommyknockers are real."

"Ye mean," Ruby asked with awe, "like haints?"

"Haunts," Hildy automatically corrected her cousin. "And I've told you a thousand times there aren't any such things. That's just mountain superstition."

"Ain't so!" Ruby flared. "Haints is real!"

Jack said, "I don't know about haints or haunts, but I know my father believed in tommyknockers, and so do I. They tried to warn him, but I guess he didn't listen."

Jack lifted the barbed wire so the girls could climb through the fence onto the dump site. Hildy eased through first and straightened up to see an ore car dump a load of rocks well out in the field.

As the car headed back toward the headframe, Jack suggested, "Let's go look through that pile just dumped. Nobody's had a chance to pick through it, so maybe we can find a few little pieces with gold in them."

The girls followed the boy with his Cornish miner's lunch pail. Hildy's mind was still on the startling things Jack had said about what happened to his father. She heard the sound of a motor coming up fast behind her and spun around.

A huge black dump truck bore down on them. Two men rode in the cab. The balding, heavyset driver leaned out the cab window. He had a very red face. "Hey, you kids!" he roared. "Whatcha think you're doin'?"

Hildy joined Ruby and Jack in looking up at the driver who halted the truck beside them.

Jack replied, "Nothing, mister, just picking up a few—"

"You ain't pickin' up nothin'!" the driver shouted. He jerked the door open and jumped to the ground. The second man also leaped down. He was a burly man with powerful chest and shoulders. He started around the front of the truck as the driver yelled, "You young punks get outta here pronto while the gettin's good!"

Jack tried again, "Mister, I come here lots—"

"Get outta here, I said!" The man took a menacing step toward the boy, who stepped back.

Hildy urged, "Come on, you two!" She turned toward the fence again. "It's not worth getting into trouble over some old rocks."

As the three friends retreated toward the fence, the driver and his helper began to hurriedly load broken rocks into the truck.

"Wonder why they chased us off?" Jack mused. "That's nothing but old waste rock from the mine."

Hildy said, "What are they going to do with it?"

"Who keers?" Ruby answered. "Let's git away from them fellers. They look downright mean an' ugly."

That night at the secret meeting, Hildy looked at Spud, her

father, Uncle Nate, and Brother Ben. She was eager to tell all that had happened to her since last night's meeting, but Nate began unexpectedly by telling about his first day in the mine.

"The Cornishmen all wear what they call 'come-to-ee and go-forth-ee' boots and clothes. We changed out of those into our work clothes, took our metal lunch buckets, and carbide lamps on our hats, then rode down the shaft on man-skips to where the miners went to work on a quartz vein. Man-skips are open iron vehicles that ride on inclined rails operated by cables. They carry miners into the mine and back to the surface. Anyway, some miners blast with dynamite and—"

Hildy flinched, making Nate pause to look at her.

"You okay?" he asked.

"Uh . . . oh, yes!"

Her uncle looked doubtful. "For a second, I thought something happened to you. Sure you're all right?"

"I'm all right," Hildy assured him.

Ruby exclaimed, "It was when ye mentioned dynamite that plumb upset her, Daddy! Would ye mind a-waitin' to finish yore story whilst Hildy tells about what Jack Tremayne said?"

When the others agreed, Hildy repeated Jack's belief that his father's death was not an accident.

Spud and the three men frequently interrupted to ask questions and offer opinions, especially about the possibility that there was a relationship between Garrett Kayne's firing and his fight with Jack's father.

Finally Ruby changed the subject. "Hildy, tell the part about them two jaspers in the truck a-runnin' us off this afternoon."

When Hildy had done that, Spud and the three men discussed the two truckers' possible motives, but nobody had any solid ideas. The conversation again returned to Jack's belief that his father's death was intentional.

Finally the old ranger said, "I'll check with my law-enforcement contacts tomorrow and see what they think. Joe and Nate, would you listen where you're working to see if you can hear anything about that? Among us, we'll see if we can discover the truth about this man's death."

Spud suggested, "All of us should try to think why Jack and the girls were ordered away from the rock dump, too."

Ruby said, "Y'all didn't let Hildy finish tellin' what else happened las' night an' today."

"Last night?" Hildy's father exclaimed. "You were asleep in your room—weren't you?"

"Not all the time, Daddy," Hildy admitted.

"You went out, alone?" her father asked sharply.

She nodded. "I didn't want to wake you—"

He interrupted in a quiet voice that showed controlled anger and concern. "We'll talk about this later. Right now, tell us what happened."

Hildy told about leaving her room and following Trey, then being chased by him and Casper Cobb.

When Hildy paused, Ruby prompted, "Tell about what Skeezix done las' night and what he said this mornin'."

Hildy nodded and explained how the old railroader had saved her from her pursuers last night. She looked at her father and added, "I was going to tell you this morning, but you'd already gone to work."

He said, "Let's hear about what Skeezix said today."

Hildy quickly repeated the old railroader's opinion that Trey Granger was carrying gold, which he'd left at the white house.

Ruby summarized for her cousin. "So Hildy an' me, we went up and looked at that house, but we didn't see no name on the mailbox, and we didn't want to ask the neighbors, so we don't know who lives thar."

"I'll go watch the place tonight," Spud volunteered, "and see if any more gold's left there. Maybe find out who lives—"

"No, ye don't!" Ruby snapped, turning to face him. "Me'n Hildy air a-gonna do that by our lonesomes!"

"Whoa, now!" Ruby's father said firmly. "I expect Joe and me'll have something to say about that."

Hildy's father stood up. "That's right, Nate. After what Hildy did last night and what happened today, I'm satisfied both these girls can get into serious trouble from which we can't protect them—at least, not in the daytime when we're all apart from each other."

He turned to his daughter. "I want you to return home as soon as possible."

"What?" Hildy cried, jumping to her feet. "We all agreed to go home together Saturday night!"

"That was before we had reason to worry about your safety."

Ruby's father also stood. "I agree with you, Joe. I'm sending Ruby home too."

Ruby squawked in protest. "Ye cain't do that!"

Nate Konning said evenly but firmly, "I love you too much to let you stay here, honey." He turned to the old ranger. "I know it's a mighty big thing to ask, but Joe and me'd be obliged if you could take these girls home as soon as possible."

"I'll first have to let my law-enforcement contacts know where I'm going," Ben answered.

Hildy, still staggered emotionally by the surprise decision, exclaimed, "But that won't give us time to tell Jack! We're to meet him again tomorrow after school."

"I'll tell him," Spud volunteered.

"Ye stay outta this!" Ruby cried. She turned to look up at her father. "Please! Cain't we at least do somethin' else afore y'all ship Hildy an' me home?"

"Like what?" Nate asked.

"Well, like—" Ruby faltered and turned to Hildy. "Jump in an' he'p me out some! What'd we want most?"

Hildy's mind reeled with the shock of being sent home. She tried to think how to answer her cousin. What did she want most?

If we go home before the highgraders are caught, Mr. Farnham won't have any money from the mine to build the hospital. Then Gladys Cassell will have died in vain.

Hildy forced her spinning thoughts to stop and focus. "How about Ruby and me watching that white house tonight? Daddy, maybe you or Uncle Nate or Brother Ben could stay nearby and watch us so we'd be safe."

Joe Corrigan started to shake his head, but the old ranger

spoke up quickly. "Since I've got the only car, I wouldn't mind driving over to watch. Spud could ride along."

Hildy breathed a sigh of relief. "Oh, thank you, Brother Ben!"

An hour later the cousins were pressed against the trunk of a big silver maple just up the street from the white Victorian house on Hardluck Hill. Ben was parked a block up the street at the top of the hill. He had wanted the girls to stay with him and Spud where it would be warmer, but they didn't want to be so far from the white house.

The October night air had a decided bite, and both girls were soon shivering in spite of having brought sweaters. Several cars climbed the hill, but none slowed or stopped until about an hour had passed.

Then another car ground steadily up the hill, slowed, and stopped. Its headlights went out and the door opened. By the faint glow of the distant streetlight at the corner below, Hildy made out the shape of a man as he stepped up on the high curb.

Ruby whispered, "That ain't Trey. This guy ain't tall enough."

"Shh! He might hear—duck!" Hildy cried as a car turned the corner at the top of the hill and started down. Its headlights threw the girls' shadows onto the man on the curb.

Hildy and Ruby instinctively jerked their heads back and pressed their bodies against the tree trunk.

Ruby whispered, "I got a glimpse of that feller with the sack! It's Garrett Kayne!"

"I saw," Hildy whispered back as the car passed and darkness again settled over everything.

"Ye reckon he seen us?"

"Shh!" Hildy held her breath and listened. She heard rapid footsteps on the concrete sidewalk.

"He's a-comin', Hildy! What're we a-gonna do?"

Before she could answer, the miner's voice seemed to thunder out of the darkness. "I see you hiding behind that tree! Come out right now!"

Chapter Nine

A MYSTERIOUS DISAPPEARANCE

Thursday Night

Hildy grabbed her cousin's hand in the darkness as Garrett Kayne's rapid footsteps came closer. "Run toward Brother Ben!" Hildy cried hoarsely, starting to race uphill.

"Stop!" Kayne's voice commanded behind them.

The girls kept running as headlights at the crest of Hardluck Hill flashed on. Hildy heard Brother Ben's big Packard engine roar to life. At the same instant, the vehicle shot toward the girls.

As the Packard's headlights bore down on them, Hildy glanced back at their pursuer. "He's gaining!" she panted. "Run faster!"

"I'm a-runnin' muh heart out now! If'n Brother Ben don't git here fast—!"

"Stop, I said!" Kayne's voice was closer, but the cousins sprinted on up the steep sidewalk.

Seconds later, the big yellow car cut sharply across the street and braked hard alongside the girls. When the Packard's headlights passed, Hildy could barely see Brother Ben's big white cowboy hat where he sat tall and straight behind the wheel.

"You're safe, girls!" he assured them.

Hildy glanced behind her. Garrett Kayne's car backed rapidly away from the curb without its lights. The tires squealed as the driver jerked the car across to the right lane, rocked it danger-ously almost to the point of tipping over, then straightened it and bolted back down the street. Only then did the headlights come on.

"That whar close!" Ruby gasped, leaning to look into the driver's side. "Thankee, Brother Ben!"

He nodded, saying, "My door won't open against this high curb. Go around to the other side, and Spud'll let you in."

Minutes later the girls finished recounting their latest scary experience as Ben stopped his car at the Shamrock Rooming House, where Ruby and her father were staying. Ben turned around to face the girls in the back seat.

"You're sure it was Garrett Kayne?" the old ranger asked Hildy, who was directly behind him.

"No doubt about it."

Ben mused softly, "Hmm. I'll have to check out his back-ground tomorrow."

"You can't," Spud reminded him. "You're driving the girls back to . . . ouch! Ruby, watch what you're doing!" He rubbed his arm, which had been draped on the back of the seat. "That hurt!"

"I meant fer it to!" Ruby replied sharply. "I'll pinch ye harder next time ye say anythin' about that!"

"Easy, Ruby," Hildy said. "It's not Spud's fault our fathers want us to go home."

The old ranger shoved his cowboy hat back farther on his head. "Let's see. Jack Tremayne told you girls that Kayne was the last man to see his father alive, but that doesn't make sense."

"Why not?" Hildy asked.

"Jack's father fired Kayne earlier, and then Kayne picked a fight with Mr. Tremayne downtown that night. So how could

Kayne have been back in the mines after that?"

Hildy volunteered, "We'll ask Jack . . . oops! Someone's coming!"

Hildy peered past her cousin and Spud as a young man with shiny black hair, neatly parted in the middle and slicked down, stopped beside the car, a cigarette in his hand.

Ruby said, "That's the night clerk at the rooming house."

The young man bent and asked, "Ruby, is that you?" When she nodded, he continued. "I thought so. I just came out for a smoke, when I saw your face by the streetlight here.

"Excuse me," he continued, still holding the unlit cigarette, "but did your father find you?"

Hildy felt a sudden sense of alarm as her cousin said through the car window, "He knows whar I was."

"He does?" the clerk asked.

"Why d'ye look so surprised?" Ruby demanded.

"Well, a man came in to the desk a while ago and said he had a message for your father. I told him where your rooms were, so he went down the hall. A couple minutes later, they both came hurrying out. Your father didn't stop, but he asked me to send a message over to Mrs. Callahan's Room and Board to a Joe Corrigan."

Hildy sucked in her breath sharply at mention of her father's name as Ruby cried, "What kinda message?"

"That's what I was trying to tell you," the clerk explained. "He said the man had just brought word that you were lost or—"

"Me?" Ruby interrupted.

The clerk nodded. "Lost or in trouble—I didn't rightly understand which, because, like I said, your father didn't slow up but just blurted it to me as he went out with that guy."

Ruby asked, "Who was this here man?"

"Sorry, I never saw him before."

"They ain't come back?"

"No. Been an hour or so by now, I guess. But I did send a kid over to Mrs. Callahan's with the message."

Ruby whirled around in the car to face the others. "Somethin's happened to muh daddy! We got to find him!"

"Easy, now," Hildy said, reaching out and putting both arms around her cousin. "It's going to be all right."

Ben raised his voice. "Thanks, mister."

As the clerk turned away and lit his cigarette, the old ranger said softly, "We'd better get over to see Joe right away. Maybe Nate's with him."

On the short drive, Hildy felt shivers pass over Ruby's body.

"Oh, please, God!" Ruby whispered so low that Hildy barely heard the words. "Don't let nothin' happen to muh daddy!"

Hildy was concerned about what might have happened to her uncle, but she was surprised to hear Ruby pray. Ruby didn't care much about religion, even if she was a preacher's kid.

Ruby raised her face slightly so her cheek was against Hildy's. Hildy felt a tear transfer itself from Ruby's face to hers.

Ruby said softly, "Hildy, I got me a turr'ble, turr'ble feelin'!"

As the Packard's headlights hit the front of Mrs. Callahan's Room and Board, Hildy breathed a sigh of relief. Her father had obviously been waiting for them. He shoved the front door open and ran to the Packard as it nosed into the curb.

"Ruby!" he exclaimed. "You're all right!"

"Shore I am!" she said, as Spud opened the door and stepped out so Ruby could climb out of the back seat. Straightening up, she asked anxiously, "But whar's muh daddy, Uncle Joe? You seen him?"

Joe Corrigan shook his head as Hildy also climbed out of the car. Ben came around from the driver's side to complete the little gathering on the curb.

Hildy's father answered Ruby. "No, I haven't. I was getting ready for bed when some boy brought a message from Nate that something had happened to you."

"I'm fine. We're all fine." Her voice rose to a wail. "But whar's muh daddy?"

The old ranger spoke reassuringly, "We'll find him. But we've got to know some things first. Joe, what happened after you got the note?"

"I knew where Ruby was supposed to be—with Hildy. And you and Spud watching after them. But I figured something had gone wrong, so I grabbed a coat and ran up to that white house. Nearly scared me to death when I got there, because none of you were there. So I ran back down here. Haven't been back two minutes. Ben, what's going on?"

Hildy glanced at the old ranger, who took a slow breath but didn't answer.

Ruby's voice rose in the night air. "Somebody done kidnapped muh daddy!"

Hildy stepped over and again put her arms around her cousin, who was shaking. "We don't know that!" Hildy said softly but firmly. "Maybe it's all a mistake."

"It ain't no sich a-thing!" Ruby almost shrieked, her eyes bright with tears. "They done kidnapped him, I betcha, an' we got to find him—fast!"

Ben said firmly, "Don't be so hasty, Ruby! Let's all go inside where we can think this through."

Inside Hildy's room, a hurried council was held. Hildy tried to comfort her cousin, but Ruby was too upset. She kept her voice down, but she was crying freely and pacing the floor, moaning to herself.

Finally, Hildy's father and the old ranger decided on a plan. All five people squeezed into the Packard and drove back to the boardinghouse where Ruby and her father had lodgings. A check with the desk clerk showed that Nate had not returned. Ben asked for a description of the man who had gone out with Nate.

The clerk stroked his chin thoughtfully. "He was kind of bald, middle-aged, with a red face."

Hildy and Ruby looked at each other and exclaimed together, "The truck driver!"

Back in the car, the girls described in detail the man who had chased them and Jack away from the dump that afternoon.

Hildy's father and the old ranger agreed that although they couldn't be sure, it seemed very possible that the truck driver and the man the clerk had described were the same person. Ben drove around town, hoping to spot either Nate or the red-faced truck driver.

After some fruitless searching, Ben said he'd drive to the police station and enlist the help of some officers.

"Seems like the only thing we can do," Hildy's father said. "But it's getting late, and these girls can't help us there. So why don't we drop them off at Mrs. Callahan's? They'll be safe until we get back."

Ruby almost shrieked, "I cain't sleep a wink! Lemme stay with y'all 'til we find muh daddy!"

Her uncle shook his head. "Sorry, Ruby. There might be trouble. It's safer if you girls stay behind."

The old ranger agreed, and drove the girls back to Mrs. Callahan's Room and Board. Hildy kissed her father and told him to be careful and come back as soon as possible. Spud left with the men.

Hildy sat on the edge of her bed and patted the place beside her. "Sit here with me, Ruby," she urged.

Ruby shook her head. "I got to be alone awhile. Do ye mind?"

"It might help you to talk, but if you'll feel better alone, go into Daddy's room and close the door." Hildy motioned to the adjoining room.

"Reckon I'll do that," Ruby said, walking through the connecting door and closing it behind her.

Hildy could heard her cousin pacing the bare wooden floor. She rose and stood by the window, trying to reason out what had happened to her uncle, but it was useless. She told herself, *Kidnapping Uncle Nate doesn't make sense! In fact, none of this makes sense!*

Then Hildy heard the bedspring squeak in her father's room and knew that Ruby had either finally sat down or was lying on the bed. Then all was quiet. *Maybe she's asleep,* Hildy thought.

She couldn't sleep herself, and time passed slowly. She spent it in murmured prayer. Finally, wondering what was taking her father so long, she lay down on her bed and stared at the ceiling.

One thing's for sure, she told herself with mixed feelings of relief and concern. *Unless Uncle Nate's found, Ruby and I won't be going home tomorrow morning.*

The single overhead light shining in Hildy's eyes bothered her, so she reached for the string at the head of the bed and pulled it. The brass-colored chain clinked gently against the bare bulb. The light went out, and darkness settled over the room.

What's keeping Daddy and the others so long? she asked herself with rising anxiety.

She turned her head on the pillow so she could see out the window. Outside, life in Quartz City continued. Raucous laughter and music came faintly through the darkness from a bar down the street. The narrow-gauge rails clicked where cars were being moved along them. The small locomotive's bell clanged.

Everything seemed very normal, although something was terribly wrong. Hildy sighed and turned her head away from the window. The streetlight made a pale path of light across her bed to the door.

She heard a tiny click in the stillness, and her heart leaped. She rose quickly and started toward the door, then stopped, and sucked in her breath.

Slowly and quietly, the knob was turning.

Chapter Ten

ANOTHER SCARE AND A WARNING

Late Thursday Night

As Hildy watched the white porcelain doorknob turning, her heart began to race with fear.

For a second she thought about running into the other room to alert her cousin. Then the outer door opened slightly, allowing the electric bulb in the hallway to cast a square of light into the darkened room where Hildy stood. At the same instant a man's shadow fell into the light.

"Daddy!" Hildy cried out with relief as the hallway light illuminated the right side of her father's face. She ran around the bed and into his arms. "Oh, Daddy! You scared me!" She added quickly, "Did you find Uncle Nate?"

"We found him." Joe Corrigan's voice sounded tired. "He's a little worse for wear, but he'll be all right. Ben and Spud are with him at the police station."

"Police? What happened?"

"I may as well tell you and Ruby at the same time. Where is she?"

Ruby burst through the inner door from the other bedroom as Hildy pulled the string, turning on the light in her room. Hildy saw the worried look on her father's face as he reached out and pulled both girls into his arms.

"Ruby, your father's going to be all right, but he's banged up some where a couple of men worked him over."

"How bad is he?" Ruby cried, her eyes wide with fright and concern.

"He hurts, but no permanent damage."

"What happened, Uncle Joe?"

"As you probably guessed, the man the rooming house clerk told us about tricked Nate into going with him by lying about you. When Nate got to a little shack by the railroad, he realized what was happening and tried to turn back. But that red-faced guy and another who came out of the shack grabbed him, dragged him inside, tied him up and—"

"Where is he?" Ruby asked wildly, breaking out of her uncle's arms. "I've got to see him!"

"He's talking to the police right now."

"Take me thar! Please, Uncle Joe!"

Hildy's father shook his head. "He told me not to do that, but to take you to Ben and Spud's place. They'll bring your father there as soon as possible. Grab your sweaters, and we'll walk over there. I'll tell you all about it on the way."

Walking through the late October night holding her cousin's hand, Hildy shivered as her father repeated what Ruby's father had told him.

"The men wanted to know what Nate was up to. He tried saying he was a part-time preacher who worked when and where he could, but they didn't believe him. They seemed to think he was planning to steal gold from the mine and—"

"Muh Daddy, steal?" Ruby interrupted, eyes blazing. "He wouldn't steal nothin'! 'Sides, I reckon they're a-stealin' gold and don't want nobody cuttin' in on it!"

"Let Daddy finish," Hildy told her.

"That's about all Nate told us when we found him staggering along by the railroad tracks."

"How'd he get there?" Hildy asked.

"Funny thing," her father answered. "Seems those men heard a sound outside and went to investigate. They'd no sooner gone out one door of that shack when an old man slipped in the back, cut Nate's bonds, and motioned for him to follow."

"What old man?" Hildy asked, thinking immediately of Skeezix.

"Nate said he'd never seen him. Anyway, the old fellow didn't say a word, but led Nate out the same door he'd come through and out along some boxcars where it was real dark. Nate started toward a streetlight, then looked back to thank the old man, but he was gone."

Hildy said, "I wonder if it was Skeezix? Did Uncle Nate say how this old man was dressed?"

"No, but we'll ask him when he gets to the Miner's Hotel, where Ben and Spud have been staying. We'll wait inside because they'll be along directly."

Entering the small lobby of what once had been a second-rate hotel, Hildy wrinkled her nose at the smell coming from the brass spittoons. There was also the lingering odor of perspiration that clung to the old, sagging upholstered chairs, although nobody else was in the room. The floral wallpaper was peeling and the ceiling was cracked.

The cousins were too excited to sit down, so they paced and talked until the Packard pulled up out front. Ruby dashed outside to greet her father. Hildy started to follow, but her father gently held her back as Ben and Spud walked into the hotel. Hildy's father explained that Nate and Ruby needed a moment alone.

When Nate Konning entered the lobby, he was stooped over and held his ribs with his right hand. He had his left arm around his daughter's waist. By the single light bulb hanging from the ceiling behind what had obviously once been the front desk, Hildy saw that her uncle's face was puffy and discolored.

He sat down with a low moan on one of the ancient couches and quickly repeated what had happened to him, adding details

Joe Corrigan hadn't known. He concluded, "From the description you kids gave, I'd guess those men were the same two who
ran you off at the rock dump."

The old ranger had taken off his cowboy hat and gingerly sat
down on a chair facing Nate. "I've asked myself," Ben began,
"how this all ties together."

As Hildy and the others looked at him expectantly, he continued. "Suppose that ore car you girls saw dumped wasn't just
waste rock from the mine? Suppose it was gold-bearing quartz
deliberately emptied where those two men were waiting for it?"

Hildy's face lit up with understanding. "You mean, maybe
that's how the stolen gold is being removed from the mine?"

The old ranger nodded and gave his moustache a flip with
the back of his right forefinger. "Don't you agree it's a possibility?"

After a brief discussion, they all agreed. Instead of sneaking
gold out in small amounts, the thieves might be taking out gold-
bearing quartz in ore cars as waste rock, then promptly picking
it up and taking it to some distant stamp mill. There it would
be crushed and the gold removed.

The old ranger stood and replaced his hat. "If that's the case,
it means somebody in authority has to be heading up the ring
of highgraders."

"Somebody like a shift boss?" Hildy asked quickly, following
Brother Ben's thoughts. "Someone like Garrett Kayne, who took
that job after John Tremayne's death?"

Ben nodded, and Ruby exclaimed, "Hey! We plumb fergot
to tell y'all what Kayne done to Hildy an' me tonight! Or woulda,
if'n it hadn't been for Brother Ben."

"And Spud," Hildy added quickly.

Ruby ignored mention of the freckled boy. "Hey!" she cried,
jumping up and facing the others. "I think we air about to solve
this here mystery of the highgrading!"

"Whoa, now, Ruby!" the old ranger cautioned. "We're making headway, I think, but we're a powerful long way from having
any evidence."

Hildy asked, "What do you think we should do?"

"I guess the first thing is to talk to Matt Farnham's mine superintendent, Leith Cowan. But I'm not anxious to do that."

"Why not?" Ruby asked. "Mr. Farnham trusts him. Don't ye?"

Ben settled his cowboy hat on his full head of white hair before answering. "It isn't that I don't trust Leith Cowan. I guess it's just that I was a lawman so long I'm naturally careful, remembering something the Bible says."

"What's that?" Hildy asked.

"Well, do you remember when Samuel was looking at all of Jesse's sons to crown one king?" When Hildy nodded, Ben continued, "When Samuel saw Jesse's first son, Samuel thought he was the one God wanted."

Ruby said, "But that warn't so! Even I know that David was made king!"

"That's right, Ruby," Ben said. "But do you remember what God said to Samuel to show why the one he thought would be chosen wasn't God's choice?"

"I ain't been to Sunday school all that much," she admitted.

Nate quoted quietly, "The Lord told Samuel not to look on the face or even the height or stature because 'the Lord seeth not as man seeth; for man looketh on the outward appearance, but the Lord looketh on the heart.' "

"Exactly!" Ben answered. "So because none of us can look on the heart, I'm just naturally careful."

Hildy's father looked at Nate. "What about you? Shouldn't you go home with the girls tomorrow?"

Nate shook his head. "I've ridden horses when I was stove up some, and I've herded sheep when I didn't feel too hot, so I'm going back into the mines tomorrow."

Ruby squawked in protest, but her father was firm: "Besides helping find out who's stealing Matt Farnham's gold, I want to win at least one convert among those miners," he explained. "If my prayers are answered, somebody's heart is being softened right now to be that person."

Ruby frowned, then said just as firmly, "I don't keer much about no converts, Daddy. But if'n ye stay, I'm a-gonna stay with ye! Ain't no way I'm a-gonna be off down in the valley whilst yo're up here like this."

Hildy saw an opportunity. "She's right! And I've got to stay with her. Now that people have seen us all together, maybe Spud could stay with us tomorrow."

Spud said that was fine with him. Hildy smiled but Ruby made a face, which nobody else seemed to notice except Hildy.

After a short discussion, the fathers reluctantly agreed. Hildy smiled with relief.

Ruby also smiled, saying, "That means we'uns kin talk with Jack tomorrer!"

Nate warned, "Following Ben's rule about looking on the heart, you girls should be careful what you say to Jack—or anybody."

"Jack's a good kid! I trust him," Hildy said.

"I didn't say you shouldn't!" Nate protested. "I'm just saying we should all be careful who we talk to, and don't say too much. Whoever's behind this highgrading plays rough." He gingerly touched his battered face. "And if Jack's right about his father, maybe these people won't stop at a beating or a warning."

Ruby shrugged. "Reckon yo're right, Daddy, but I'm daid certain Jack kin be trusted."

"Probably can," the old ranger replied, "But suppose he's not telling you the truth about his father's death? Wait! Before you get upset, remember I'm only trying to get everyone to be careful until we know for sure who's involved in this highgrading."

That led into a review of all that had happened since they'd arrived in Quartz City. It seemed certain that Trey Granger, Casper Cobb, and Garrett Kayne were in on the underhanded dealings. So were the two men who had chased Jack and the girls out of the dump area, plus whoever lived in the white house on Hardluck Hill. Ben said that tomorrow he would check on that house with his police contacts.

With a final word of caution from the old ranger, the meeting broke up. Back at Mrs. Callahan's, Hildy was so excited she couldn't sleep. She tossed on her bed, thoughts turbulent as a tornado, long after she heard her father snoring in the next room. Finally, she pulled the string and turned on the light. She took the Bible her grandfather had given her and read for a while.

Using the small concordance at the back, she found the verse Brother Ben had referred to. Hildy turned to the first book of Samuel and read the story.

Closing the Bible, Hildy placed it on the nightstand and turned out the light. She closed her eyes and was almost asleep when she heard a faint noise.

What's that? she asked herself, sitting up in bed.

She turned toward the outer door, half expecting to see the doorknob again slowly turning. She breathed a sigh of relief when it remained perfectly still.

Then she saw something slide under the door. She heard the footsteps of someone hurrying away down the hall. It sounded as though they were walking on tiptoe.

With heart racing, Hildy threw back the musty covers and slid out of bed. She padded barefoot across the wooden floor. At the doorway, she held her breath, then bent for a closer look by the dim glow of the streetlight filtering through the dirty window.

Looks like a piece of paper. Maybe a note.

Hildy picked it up just as she heard the outside door to the boardinghouse click shut. Still fighting a rising sense of fear, she returned to her bed and pulled the light string.

She blinked at the sudden brightness of the room, then glanced at the paper in her hand. It was crudely printed, but easy to read.

> The answer is near the second shaft entrance until Saturday morning, but it's very dangerous, so you'd better not go alone.
> A friend.

CHAPTER Eleven

THE TRAIL GROWS HOTTER

Friday Morning

With rising excitement and curiosity, Hildy reread the note. Her mind raced. *Second shaft entrance? What's that? And where? Why won't it be there after Saturday morning? How come it's dangerous? I'd better show this note to Daddy!*

She ran barefoot to his connecting bedroom door and started to knock, then paused, thinking fast: *Daddy was late getting to sleep because of what happened to Uncle Nate, and he has to be up early to go to work. I'll just leave the note under his door so he'll see it when he comes out in the morning. Then he'll wake me up and we'll talk.*

In spite of her excitement, Hildy slept soundly. Upon waking, she leaped out of bed and ran to speak to her father. He'd apparently not seen the piece of paper she'd left for him. It was still on the floor and he was at work.

Hildy ate another hurried breakfast while Mrs. Callahan clucked her tongue disapprovingly over a young girl twice sleeping late. Hildy didn't dare explain, so she listened in silence. Then she hurried to meet Ruby and Spud. She showed them the note and told how she'd gotten it.

Ruby pondered the signature. "A friend? Hmm, ye reckon it was really left by a friend?"

Hildy shrugged. "It's hard to say."

A sharp wind had risen during the night and now was blowing leaves from the trees and making them scurry down the street like so many brown rats. Spud tugged his aviator's cap down a little tighter. "Only possible friends we've got around here are Mr. Cowan, Skeezix, and Jack," he said.

"How about Mrs. Callahan?" Hildy asked. "She's nice, but she didn't say anything at breakfast."

Ruby said, "I kin think of another possibility. Ye reckon there's somebody else we don't know about, but who thinks of us as friends?"

"Like who?" Spud challenged.

Ruby squirmed and said defensively, "Offhand, I don't know. I jist asked if'n y'all thought it was a possibility."

Spud suggested, "We could talk to both Skeezix and Jack and try to find out if it was one of them. And maybe to Mr. Cowan."

Ruby said sharply, "Oh, shore! Jist walk up to each of 'em, show the note, and ask, real polite-like, 'Did ye write this?' What I'd ruther do is find out what was meant by a second shaft. I ain't heard o' no sich thing since we been here."

"We could ask Skeezix about that right now," Spud said. "He's always near the depot. We wouldn't have to tell him why we want to know."

"I want to show it to my daddy first," Hildy replied. "Then we could ask Skeezix if he's ever heard of a second shaft."

"And if he doesn't know," Spud added, "we can ask Jack when we meet him after school."

"Good idee!" Ruby agreed. "Meanwhile, 'member to keep a sharp eye out so none o' them mean men ketch us alone. I reckon they won't bother us none if'n we stick together. I don't want nobody to git hurt like happened to muh daddy."

"Does that include me?" Spud asked.

Ruby glowered at him. "I ain't never cottoned much to ye,

but I wouldn't wish ye or nobody else any pain."

Hildy walked between Spud and Ruby to the depot. She was disappointed that her father wasn't in sight. The building was deserted except for a lone man sitting behind the ticket counter. He said that Joe Corrigan had been sent to sweep out a train. When Hildy asked which train, she was told she couldn't go there even if he told her, which he wasn't going to do.

As Hildy, Ruby, and Spud left the depot and started looking for Skeezix, Hildy looked around to make sure nobody could overhear her. "Do you suppose he's sweeping out the gold train?"

Ruby's eyes brightened. "Hey, maybe that's it! 'Member what Skeezix said about them a-gittin' a gold train made up for a run to Colfax?"

Spud nodded. "Makes sense. Otherwise, why wouldn't that man let us see Mr. Corrigan?"

Before Ruby or Spud could reply, Skeezix rose from behind a stack of crates near the end of the loading platform. "Top o' the morning to you all!" he greeted them.

After all three returned the greeting, Hildy tried to think of a way to ask if the old man had helped her Uncle Nate escape from his captors last night.

Ruby was more direct. "Skeezix," she began, looking steadily at him, her voice soft. "If yo're the one that he'ped muh daddy las' night to git away from them thar men that beat up on him, I'm plumb obliged."

"Who, me?" the retired railroad man replied in mock innocence. His voice took on a bitter edge. "I already told you that everybody says I'm jist an old codger that nobody wants around." He winked at Ruby and whispered, " 'Course I done it, but don't tell nobody." He raised his voice and abruptly changed the subject. "What brings you three this way so early today?"

Hildy explained that she was looking for her father, but he was cleaning up a train somewhere that she wasn't allowed to go.

"Gold train, most likely," Skeezix said. "I told you before that they were getting it ready to take a shipment of bullion to Colfax. The railroad tries to keep such shipments secret so's they won't get robbed—not that anybody's ever tried."

Hildy wanted to know more about that, but Ruby was anxious to pursue another topic. "Ye ever hear tell of a second mine shaft?"

Skeezix asked thoughtfully, "Why do you ask?"

"Cain't say. But did ye?"

The old railroader was silent a moment. "Well, it's not generally known, but the Shasta Daisy's got one."

"It has?" Hildy exclaimed. "Where?"

Skeezix removed his striped railroader's cap and resettled it on his thinning hair before answering. "It's somewhere out beyond the Daisy. The headframe's fallen down in the brush, so it's hard to find." He frowned. "You kids ain't thinking of going in there, are you? Old mines are dangerous, you know."

"I've heard, but don't worry!" Hildy exclaimed. "I'm scared of such places."

"Claustrophobic," Spud explained.

Hildy wasn't frightened of most things, but she had an abnormal fear of narrow, enclosed places. She'd tried to get over it, and once had entered an underground cave, but that experience had only made her fear worse.

She asked the old railroader, "I wonder how come nobody's mentioned that other shaft?"

"Maybe because it's not really a second shaft. Actually, it was originally the opening to the Bighill Mine. That was before it was bought out by the Shasta Daisy and the underground passageways of the mines were connected. Anyway, the shaft you asked about is partially caved in, not that it matters much because everything goes in and comes out the Daisy's shaft now."

Spud asked, "How would we find this Bighill shaft?"

Skeezix shook his head. "I don't think I ought to tell you kids, 'cause if you went there and got hurt, I'd feel it was my fault."

"Please!" Ruby begged. "It's powerful important we know whar it is!"

"Sorry, kids. I can't say any more."

Hildy was disappointed, but her thoughts turned to the note that had been slid under her door. "Skeezix, do you consider us three as your friends?"

"I consider everybody my friends," he replied with a wave of both hands that seemed to take in the whole town. "I hope you kids figure I'm your friend too. But I'm still not going to tell you where that other shaft is."

As the trio walked across the railroad tracks toward the downtown section of Quartz Hill, Ruby spoke with feeling: "We'uns jist got to find that thar second shaft—an' before to-morrer mornin', 'cause then it'll be too late—though I cain't figger why."

"Me either," Hildy replied. "So that leaves only Mr. Cowan and Jack who might help us. Let's go see Mr. Cowan, because we can't see Jack until after school."

Ruby pointed. "Lookee yonder at who's walking up the street ahead of us."

Hildy stared. "It's Jack! What's he doing out of school this time of day?" She started to call out to the boy, who was going the other way, but Spud put two fingers in his mouth and whistled shrilly.

Ruby grumbled, "Ye don't hafta do that in muh ear!"

Jack turned around, waved, and ran to meet them. They jogged toward him, passing store windows filled with merchandise, totally unlike Lone River, where the Depression forced stores to have very limited stock.

As they met, Hildy introduced Jack to Spud, then asked, "Jack, why aren't you in school?"

"I had to see you!" he replied, glancing nervously around. "Been looking all over for you."

"Well, ye found us," Ruby said. "Why'd ye need to see us fer?"

Jack shot furtive looks around, then lowered his voice. "Can't talk here! You three go down the nearest alley to the right and circle back this way, but stay behind the stores. Meet me by that old corrugated garage." He hurried on.

All three friends stared after him but he didn't slow down or look back.

"Come on," Hildy urged, turning up the street again. "Let's see what this is all about."

Like countless other Gold Rush towns, Quartz Hill had narrow alleys that ran between buildings made long ago of adobe mud and glass windows fitted with solid iron shutters. These had been attempts by early residents to limit damage done by the periodic fires that swept mining communities, destroying whole towns.

Hildy walked between Spud and Ruby down the first alley.

Ruby said, "I reckon Jack's the one who slid that thar note under yore door, Hildy."

"Well," Spud added thoughtfully, "If Jack did it, is he going to tell us where the second shaft is? And will he tell us why it's dangerous?"

The trio hurried past the thin trunks of 15-foot tall Chinese trees of heaven that had taken root in the sparse dirt next to the old buildings. Seed pods that had not fallen to the ground yet vibrated ominously as the kids passed, reminding Hildy of a rattlesnake's warning.

Jack was already standing in the shelter of the garage when Hildy, Ruby, and Spud arrived. Jack motioned them in close.

"I think I know why all of you are up here," he began, looking from one to the other. "If I'm right, you're all in big trouble."

"Why?" Hildy asked.

"I began figuring it out after those two men in the truck ran you girls and me off yesterday afternoon," Jack explained. "You've been asking questions, and not the kind schoolkids from the valley would normally ask."

"So?" Ruby challenged.

"So if I'm right, and I don't try to help you, you could end up like my father."

The ominous words fell heavily on Hildy's ears. She gulped before asking in a weak voice, "You mean—we might have an 'accident' too?"

"Accident!" Jack's voice shot up. "I told you—" He hesitated, lowered his voice, and continued, "There's no sense standing here talking. You want to see something?"

"What?" Hildy asked quickly, hopefully.

"You know where the airport is?" Jack asked, still in a subdued voice.

Hildy looked at Ruby and Spud. All three shook their heads.

Jack pointed toward the eastern hills carpeted with the uniform beauty of ponderosa pines. "Head out past the Shasta Daisy. Listen for the sound of airplanes. Not many take off, but they're being repaired and tested, so they'll make enough noise that you can find the runway."

"What're we going to look for?" Hildy asked.

"I'll meet you there and show you."

Ruby asked, "Ain't ye a-comin' with us?"

Jack shook his head. "Meet me there as soon as you can, but stay out of sight. Don't go onto the runway or near the hangars. Keep on the road, go past the runway, and wait in the trees beyond the manzanita at the north end of the field." He turned and walked rapidly away.

The trio set a brisk pace that took them down the steep streets of Quartz City, past Chinatown, across the railroad tracks, and toward the mountains along a paved road. They passed the Shasta Daisy's 92-foot tall headframe, eager to hear or see an airplane. Instead, they heard only the steady thudding of the stamp mills and mining traffic going in and out of the half-dozen other mines along the road.

Hildy thought that maybe they'd somehow become lost, when a biplane roared off the runway into the windy sky, revealing the location of the airport.

A few minutes after they had slipped quietly off the roadway and into the shelter of the tall conifers, or cone-bearing evergreens, Jack appeared from the dense manzanita.

"Whew!" Hildy exclaimed. "How'd you creep up on us like that?"

"There are paths through it," Jack explained, waving casually at the crazily twisted, burgundy-colored growth. "Bears like the berries."

"B'ars?" Ruby croaked, glancing around in alarm.

Jack chuckled. "They're not out much this time of day. Anyway, they're usually not dangerous. But—" he let his words trail off and looked thoughtfully toward the distant Shasta Daisy's headframe.

"But what?" Hildy prompted.

"Come on," Jack replied. "I'll show you."

The three followed the miner's son through stands of evergreen Scotch bloom thick with long, dry seed pods.

Hildy asked, "Where're we going?"

Jack answered over his shoulder. "To a mine shaft."

Being claustrophobic, the mere thought caused a sudden, sickening sensation in Hildy's stomach. "Uh, Jack, you're not thinking of going into it, are you?"

"You scared?" he asked.

Hildy gulped. "Plenty!"

Jack stopped and looked steadily at her, then at Ruby and Spud. "How about you two?" he asked.

"I'm not scared if we have lights," Spud said.

"Same here," Ruby agreed.

Hildy felt awkward and embarrassed, but her fear was real. "I'm sorry," she said softly.

"No problem," the miner's son decided. "You can stay outside while they go in with me." He turned and led the way again.

"What're you going to show us, uh, them?" Hildy asked.

"Where—and how—my father died," Jack replied grimly.

CHAPTER
TWELVE

DANGER DOWN BELOW

Friday Mid-morning

Hildy gasped in surprise. "I thought your father died in the Shasta Daisy!"

"He did," Jack answered, "but the security guards there won't let us in through the main shaft, so we have to enter this way. This used to be the Bighill Mine before it was sold to the Daisy people. They connected both mines underground years ago and stopped using this entrance. Almost nobody knows about this shaft, but my father did, and took me in a few times. Come on."

Hildy fought down a sense of rising panic that was as strong as her claustrophobia. "Wait!" she cried, remembering what Skeezix had said. "I thought this entrance had caved in."

Jack frowned. "Part of it has. But how'd you know about that?"

Hildy glanced uncertainly at Spud and Ruby. "A friend told us," she said evasively. "He also said this shaft's not safe."

"No mine's really safe," Jack replied. "There have been fires, cave-ins, gasses, and all kinds of other disasters that have killed miners."

"How many—uh—things have happened like what happened to your father?" Hildy asked.

"Call it what it is!" Jack snapped. "Murder! So far's I know, there's never been another in the mines."

Hildy tried to sound reasonable. "Then how can you be so sure that's what happened to him?"

"I want you to see for yourselves what I know. My father didn't die in an accident, and I want whoever killed him to be caught and punished!"

Spud seemed puzzled. "How will seeing the site where it happened make us believe what you do? After all, lots of other people must have been there and seen everything. Like the people who found your father, and maybe the coroner or sheriff's department."

"They're blind, that's why!" Jack's voice rose angrily. "Either they're scared, or bought off, or they just plain can't see."

His voice softened. "I can't really blame them, though. I was there just once, right after it happened, and I didn't see anything suspicious either. Later, I got to thinking of things my father had said, and then I remembered something I'd seen in the mine where they found Dad.

"I tried to get the mine people to let me go back down there to take another look before I said anything, but they wouldn't let me. And I didn't dare tell them, because whoever did it might try to do me in too."

"Ahh!" Ruby scoffed, "nobody'd hurt ye! Why, yo're jist a kid like us, and I've heard them Cornish miners air real upstandin' men. They wouldn't put up with nothin' like that."

"They would if they didn't know the truth of it," Jack explained with quiet assurance.

"You mean, another—'accident'?" Hildy guessed.

The boy nodded. "Same thing could happen to you three if whoever did my father in guessed you were trying to help me. I got to thinking about that in the night, and it scared me. So I ditched school to find you."

"And that's why you had us meet you behind the stores,"

Spud guessed, "and then come alone out here to meet you."

"That's why. Since I don't know who's behind this, I can't take any more chances than necessary."

"What did you remember seeing down there?" Hildy asked, still trying to keep from having anyone enter the unsafe second shaft.

"Can't tell you. Got to see it for yourself. I'd have gone by myself, but I'll need witnesses to prove I'm right. Boy, I tell you, it's made me mighty scared, knowing that whoever did it might be watching me! But I didn't dare trust anyone, not until now."

"How do you know you can trust us?" Hildy asked.

"Just a hunch," Jack answered. "That and the fact they're going to blow this shaft shut tomorrow."

"Who said so?" Ruby demanded.

"My father told me that he'd given the powder monkey orders to do it no later than the 19th of October. That's tomorrow."

"Maybe the new shift boss changed the orders," Spud speculated.

"That's not likely, because he probably doesn't know about it. Almost nobody does. If they did, the company would be afraid some hunter or kid would stumble into the shaft and sue. The mine operators can't take a chance on that. Anyway, it was Dad's job to know all about the mine, and he knew about this.

"He also knew that there's another box of old dynamite back in one corner of a stope off this shaft. A stope is an underground excavation from which the ore has been removed."

Hildy sucked in her breath. "You mean—dynamite like the kind that caused your father's death?"

"Yes, but this powder's safe as long as nothing bothers it. Anyway," Jack continued, "Dad told Mom and me that rather than have the powder monkey move the 'sweating' sticks and risk him getting hurt, Dad figured the unstable dynamite would blow up when the powder monkey blasted the shaft shut. It'd be like getting two birds with one stone, you know.

"Besides," Jack concluded, "the powder monkey liked Dad and would do what he told him, even after he's gone. Now I'm tired of talking. Are you with me or not?"

All eyes turned on Hildy. She was embarrassed, but she wasn't foolish. She didn't want the other three to risk their lives unnecessarily. That was especially true now that she knew they'd have to go near unstable blasting powder to enter the mine.

"Jack," she asked, "what purpose will it serve to show us where your father died?"

The miner's son studied her face thoughtfully for a long moment before answering. "Because you're the only people I've ever talked to who acted as if they believed me. Besides, I'm not just doing this for myself, but for my mother and my brothers and sisters, and everybody who knew Dad. I want people to know what really happened to him, and I want his murderer caught. Because time's running out, I've decided I've got to trust you three to help me. So how about it?"

Hildy, Ruby, and Spud looked at each other.

Spud said, "I'm game."

Ruby said hastily, "Anything ye kin do, I kin." Then she paused and added, " 'Less thar's haints. Sometimes they hang around whar daid people's been, 'specially when a person didn't die natural-like."

Hildy was about to reprimand her cousin for still believing in haints, but Jack spoke first.

"We'll be safe, 'cause the tommyknockers would warn us if it wasn't."

Hildy and Spud exchanged knowing glances. Spud had a slight smile on his lips, but Hildy gave him a warning look, and the smile vanished.

"Have you been down in this shaft by yourself?" Hildy asked Jack.

"Sure!" he turned and waved toward the weathered wooden headframe that lay partially exposed in the brush. "I've brought lights and ropes and things and left them here. I kept hoping somebody would come along I could trust, and I'd be ready. So it's now or never."

He turned and pushed through the Scotch broom, stepping over rusted cables that had once hauled ore from inside the shaft to the top of the headframe.

With a shrug, Spud followed, ducking his head and throwing up both arms to protect his face from the green switches of Scotch broom.

Ruby started after the boys, then paused to look at Hildy to ask quietly. "Ye a-comin'?"

Hildy hesitated a moment. "Well, maybe I'll go inside a little way." She followed the boys, with Ruby bringing up the rear.

Ruby whispered, "Jack's the one who slid that thar note under yore door, huh?"

"Must be. He knows about this second shaft and the deadline."

"If'n I was him, I'd be plumb des'prit." Ruby was still whispering. "I mean, knowin' thar ain't no more time, and he's got to do it now, even trustin' us. Why, we ain't nothin' but strangers to him, ye know!"

Hildy turned around and laid her right forefinger across her lips. "He's stopping."

Jack walked around a live oak tree trunk and raised his voice. "Careful! The manzanita and Scotch broom have grown up so much they hide the shaft, so you could stumble in if you didn't know it's . . . Get down!" He glanced skyward while dropping quickly into the sheltering underbrush. "Get down, I said!"

Instinctively, Hildy obeyed, not understanding what was happening. She saw that Ruby and Spud had also crouched. Their eyes were lifted skyward, following Jack's gaze. Hildy looked up too.

Her heart had started to speed up at the urgency of Jack's sudden, unexpected command. She almost laughed with relief when she saw a small, high-winged cabin plane zooming low overhead, heading for the nearby airport.

The craft passed with the sound of a throttled-back engine to disappear beyond the manzanita. A moment later, dust whipped into the air, revealing the craft had landed.

Jack stood up. "Probably no one in the plane could have seen us in the brush, even if we hadn't hidden. But we can't be too careful." He motioned Hildy, Ruby, and Spud to gather around the yawning black hole marking the shaft.

Hildy could see it was partly filled with dirt and brush.

"Now," Jack continued, "let me tell you a couple things before we go down. Naturally, the man-skips the miners used to ride down and back up are long gone, so we'll have to use the ladder. It's very old and made of wood, but I've repaired some of the rungs, so I hope it's safe."

"You hope?" Hildy asked, her voice almost cracking.

"Uh-huh." Jack turned to a black oak log. He reached down and pulled brush away from the log, revealing a large dark hole. "We'll need these things." He reached in and pulled out four hard hats. Each had a small reflector light attached to the front.

"These are carbide lamps," he explained, handing them out. "They burn for about two hours without refueling. Each of you hold yours out, and I'll light it."

Jack struck a match and quickly touched it to Spud's and Ruby's lamps. Hildy heard a hissing as the carbide gas caught fire, then settled down to produce a steady flame. The polished reflector behind each lamp intensified the light.

"You've decided to come down with us, Hildy?" Jack asked, pausing before her as she held out the hat with the carbide lamp.

She couldn't answer at first. Thoughts flashed through her mind making her feel very fragile. All her instincts warned her not to even enter the mine.

Yet she wanted Jack to have justice, and she wanted to control her claustrophobia, even if she couldn't make it go away. She also wondered how helping Jack had any relationship to why she and the other five from Lone River had come to Quartz Hill. How would her next step possibly meet Mr. Farnham's goal of finding out who was highgrading his gold from the Shasta Daisy and how it was being done?

Call it a hunch, she thought, *but maybe this whole thing ties together. I've got to find out.* Aloud, she said in a small, tight voice, "Maybe just a little way down."

Jack smiled encouragingly at her and lit her carbide lamp. "Everybody put your hats on," he instructed. He turned again to the hollow log and pulled a large coil of rope from it. "Safety line," he explained.

Hildy gulped at the length of the rope. "How far down are you planning to go?" she asked.

"Just to the first drift," Jack answered. "That's a horizontal passage underground which follows a gold vein. There's a station right by the shaft—a place where the rock has been removed, like an underground room, so men and materials can be delivered or taken out.

"If you want to, Hildy, you can stay there and hold one end of the rope while the rest of us go down the drift. We'll feed the line out behind us. That's just in case we run into trouble and need to feel our way back."

Hildy's heart jumped. "You mean, like if your lights go out? Don't you have extra fuel?"

"No, but don't worry. We won't be gone long."

Hildy's mind screamed warnings against going down, but she forced herself to follow Jack, Spud, and Ruby. The ladder was old and rickety. It jiggled unsteadily under Hildy's feet as she started down after the others. Debris had partially filled the opening, barely leaving room for the ladder and the four people who cautiously worked their way down it, single file. The shaft seemed to close in tighter with each halting step down toward the first drift.

Oh, Lord! Hildy prayed silently, fighting her claustrophobia. *I'm so scared! But I can't let them go alone!*

She glanced down, her carbide lamp making Jack, Ruby, and Spud's shadows mingle so they were one giant glob. Everyone moved without speaking, so that the creaking sounds of the ladder were amplified in Hildy's ears. The darkness closed in rapidly, so thick and black it seemed to threaten the four hissing carbide lamps. A musty smell of wet earth filled Hildy's nostrils.

She glanced up with a suppressed sob as the opening above slowly grew smaller and finally faded away. The mine shaft was now in utter darkness except for the four dancing lights reflecting off the wall.

Hildy fought with all her willpower to keep from calling out, *I'm going back up!* She kept going, step by step down the ladder, which sagged, creaked and groaned. Hildy tried to ignore the sound, just as she tried not to notice the tiny splinters that pricked her hands and fingers.

Suddenly she stiffened, hearing two strange new sounds. She paused, head cocked. "Listen!" she called in a low, hoarse whisper. The word bounced back as an echo as she asked, "What's that?"

The others paused and were silent a second. "I hear it too!" Ruby said. "Sounds like water a-drippin'."

"That's what it is," Jack said from his position farthest down the ladder. "It rains a lot here in the Northern Mines area, so the water table's pretty high. In fact, all the mines would soon fill with water if they weren't pumped out.

"Naturally, this one hasn't been pumped in years, so that's why we're only going down to the first drift. It'll get wetter, but we'll be okay." He continued down the ladder with Spud and Ruby following.

Hildy started to ask about the second sound she'd heard. The words died in her mouth when her light caught a pair of tiny eyes twenty feet away. They glowed in the dark and seemed to be looking directly at her.

She sucked in her breath. "What's that?"

She didn't take her eyes off the twin bright spots but she heard the others pause.

Jack's chuckle came up to her, echoing off the shaft. "Just a rat."

"A rat!" Hildy and Ruby repeated together.

"Sure!" Jack's voice was calm and unconcerned. "Place is full of them. Ignore them and let's go. Listen!"

Hildy suppressed a shudder as she watched the big rodent disappear into the darkness. She held her breath and listened. The silence told her the others were doing the same. Hildy heard only her own breathing.

"Hear it?" Jack's voice had changed from calm to sudden concern.

Spud confessed, "I don't hear anything."

"There it is again!" Jack's voice sounded awed. "That tapping sound! It's the tommyknockers! They're warning us!"

"Ahh," Spud chided, "there's no such—"

"We've got to get out of here!" Jack blurted. "Hildy! Climb back up the ladder! Fast!"

"I don't hear any. . ." she began, then broke off, her heart jumping in alarm. She heard an ominous crack and at the same instant the ladder rung on which she stood snapped with a terrible splintering sound.

Hildy's legs shot out from under her, taking her breath away. She was falling feet first into the empty blackness below.

CHAPTER
THIRTEEN

—

A CLOSE CALL

Friday Mid-morning

"Ooooh!" Hildy cried out as she made a wild grab at the ladder. The fingers of her right hand caught the wooden rung below the one that had broken. Instinctively, she gripped it with all her might, ending her fall so abruptly that her right shoulder was nearly yanked from its socket.

That was the least of her problems, so she silently bore the pain while searching frantically with her other hand. It closed on the left upright part of the ladder. She held on, her body dangling helplessly in the air, feet flailing about in an effort to find another rung in the darkness.

Her left shoe struck Ruby in the head, knocking her hat off. The attached lamp spun crazily, making monstrous shadows that silently chased each other around the shaft.

Hildy's weight threatened to pull her fingers loose from their splintery grip. She continued to thrash about for another rung on which to rest her feet. As her weakening fingers almost let go, her toes finally touched a rung and she settled both feet on it, easing the pain in her arms and shoulders. Her trembling body collapsed against the ladder.

"Thank you, Lord!" she whispered, briefly closing her eyes. She opened them in time to see Ruby's hat hit the rocky passageway at the bottom of the shaft. The hat bounced, then the light went out.

The whole ordeal lasted only seconds, but Hildy was drained physically and emotionally.

"Hildy, answer me! Are you all right?" Spud's voice from below penetrated Hildy's frightened mind.

Hildy looked down, her light showing three very frightened faces below on the ladder. "Yes," she managed to say, surprised at how weak the word sounded.

Jack said, "Hildy, if you're okay, you've got to climb out! Can you do it?"

"I . . . think so."

Hildy lifted her head so the light showed the empty place where the broken rung had been. She reached up and stretched as far as possible beyond the missing rung. Her fingers touched, then curled around the next one up. The action made her aware that her shoulder ached and both hands had been cut in the fall.

She ignored the pain and brought her right foot up. When it stepped down on nothingness where the broken rung had been, she almost panicked. She grabbed the rung above with her other hand and pulled hard, as if she were chinning herself.

She felt a moment of terror when both feet swung free. She didn't breathe until she'd managed to bend her legs up at an awkward angle, twist her body, and lift both feet past the missing rung while feeling for the next solid one above.

"Watch out for that missing rung!" she warned the others.

"We're a-watchin'," Ruby assured her.

Hildy heard the others scramble after her. She covered the last stretch of the ladder as quickly as possible. Moments later, she reached the opening of the shaft and sprawled weakly on the ground above.

Soon Ruby, Spud, and Jack were bending anxiously over Hildy. She heard their collective sigh of relief.

"The tommyknockers tried to warn us," Jack said in an awed voice.

Hildy looked up at Jack. "I didn't hear anything."

Spud agreed. "Neither did I."

Jack protested, "But it was so plain! Ruby, you heard them, didn't you?"

"No, cain't say's I did."

Hildy wanted to say something to Jack about his imagining things and that tommyknockers were just superstition. Instead, she said, "I've had enough of mines for one day."

Ruby and Spud agreed, but Jack's face showed his anguish. "They're going to blow this place up tomorrow!" he cried. "We've got to go back down there so I can show you the proof of what happened to my father."

He took off his hat and extinguished the flame. "Tell you what. I'll run home and get a hammer and nails to fix the ladder. I can have it done in a couple hours, then we can all go down again. How about it?"

Hildy, Ruby, and Spud discussed the idea. Hildy suggested they try to find her father and talk to him first. Ruby and Spud agreed. Jack sighed, then hid the hats and rope in the hollow log. All four started walking back toward town as an airplane took off from the airport. It headed south over the pine-clad mountains.

Hildy idly followed it with her eyes as the plane grew smaller and smaller. Suddenly she frowned and stopped, staring into the sky.

Ruby asked, "Whatcha doin'?"

"I just had a thought," Hildy started to explain, then shook her head. "No, it's too wild to even mention."

She raised her eyes to the headframe rising above the Shasta Daisy Mine and changed the subject. "As long as we're passing here, let's stop in so I can ask Mr. Cowan something."

Jack protested, "I don't think that's a good idea! I'll go on home for hammer and nails while you three go to the depot and talk to Hildy's father. The sooner we get back to the mine so I can show you what I remember, the better."

Spud said, "I have to go along with you on that."

Ruby snapped, "Oh, ye do, do ye? Well, then, I'm with Hildy!"

Hildy spoke quickly to prevent her cousin and Spud from getting into another argument. "Let's compromise! You boys go together while Ruby and I stop off at the Shasta Daisy. It won't take long. Then we'll try to find Daddy."

Jack's voice showed his disappointment. "You're not saying that just to keep from going back down into the shaft with me after lunch, are you?"

Hildy thought fast. She was ashamed to admit it, but she had been terribly scared by her close call on the ladder. She took a deep breath and announced her decision. "I'm never going back into that place, and I don't think any of you should either! But if my daddy says it's okay, I'll go with you again and hold the rope while the rest of you go down. But I hope none of you will have to."

The boys accepted Hildy's decision and continued walking toward town while Hildy and Ruby approached the office at the Shasta Daisy. They gave their names to a young secretary and asked if they could see Mr. Cowan. She checked by phone, then ushered them into the superintendent's office.

"What an unexpected pleasure!" he said, coming around his desk to welcome them. "What can I do for you young ladies today?"

"Don't ask me, Mr. Cowan!" Ruby said. "Hildy's got a bee in her bonnet, but she ain't tol' me nothin' about it."

Hildy started to explain, but hesitated when she saw the mine superintendent staring at her hands. She self-consciously put them behind her back. "I had a little accident," she explained. "Nothing serious."

"I see." His voice changed. "Now, what's on your mind, Hildy?"

She thought about how to phrase the question properly. "Can you show us where they pour the melted gold into the molds to cool?"

"Sorry, but that's off limits even to friends of Matt Farnham, though he is the owner of this mine." Cowan paused, then added, "Unless, of course, you have written permission from him?"

It was a probing question, and Hildy shook her head. "No, I'm just curious."

"Any special reason?"

"No, just wondering. Well, since we can't see it, can you tell us how it's done?"

"No harm in that, I guess. Sit down." He motioned for the girls to take chairs and walked around the desk to his own chair. "Something for a school project, Hildy?"

"Maybe, but right now I'm just interested."

"I see. Well, I'd better back up a little so you'll understand the process leading up to the ingots. The other day when I gave you a tour, I showed you where the rock is crushed at the stamp mill.

"You see, sometimes gold is found in nuggets that you can carry. But most often, in hardrock mining, it's like tiny grains of sand. That's why the ore-bearing rocks from the mine have to go to the crusher. Can you hear it?"

Hildy nodded. She could feel the incessant sound as well as hear it.

"Then when the ore is crushed to sand, we discard the sand and keep what's called the free gold. This is sent on to the next step where it is combined with mercury on what's called amalgamation tables. Gold sticks to mercury, which is later removed at the cyanide plant. The gold goes to the refinery."

Hildy nodded, noticing that Ruby seemed puzzled by why her cousin wanted to know all that.

"At the refinery," the superintendent continued, "huge furnaces, heated very hot, separate the gold from any remaining residue. Then the liquid gold is poured into molds to cool. These gold bars are called ingots."

"How big are they?" Hildy interjected.

"Each weighs 89 pounds."

Ruby let out a low whistle. "Each one?"

"Each one."

"Lemme see how much one o' them's worth . . ." Ruby raised her right hand and began drawing figures in the air. "If gold's worth $35 an ounce . . ."

"It is," the mine superintendent acknowledged. "It was $20.67 from 1879 until it began to rise last year. It rose to $30 in September. Then this year the government devalued the dollar by raising the price of gold to $35 an ounce."

Ruby continued figuring in the air. "Thirty-five dollars an ounce times a pound . . ."

"Don't forget gold's weighed in troy ounces. That's 12 ounces to the pound."

Ruby nodded. "Thankee, Mr. Cowan. Twelve ounces times $35 . . ." She hesitated uncertainly.

The mine superintendent helped her out. "That comes to $420 a pound. Multiply that by 89 pounds per ingot, and the answer is $37,380 each."

"Whooeee!" Ruby whispered in awe. "Why, even *one* o' them gold bars could make a body rich!"

Hildy leaned forward, resting her tender hands on the corner of the desk. "Then these bars of solid gold are sent to the mint in San Francisco? Is that right?"

"Yes. The law says all gold must be sold to Uncle Sam. So when they're ready to ship, we put them in small canvas sacks—"

"Small canvas sacks?" Ruby interrupted.

"That's right."

Hildy was sure Ruby was thinking the same thing she was, so she shot her cousin a warning glance and gave a quick, short shake of her head.

"These gold bars go on the train, Mr. Cowan?" Hildy asked quickly.

"They could." The mine superintendent's voice held a note of caution. "Or they could go by truck or car. Naturally, the way they're shipped, the time, and how many ingots per shipment must be kept confidential."

Hildy nodded. "I understand, Mr. Cowan. Just one more question, please, and then we'll let you get back to work. Is this mine the only place that produces gold bars?"

"Oh, no. Any mine can produce them, provided they have the equipment."

Hildy stood up and smiled. "Well, thanks a lot, Mr. Cowan." She turned toward the door, with Ruby falling into step beside her.

"Just a moment, please," Cowan said, coming around the desk. "Are you girls going to be in town Sunday?"

Hildy replied, "I don't think so. But maybe. Why?"

"I want to invite you to church. Bring all your party with you. We have a gifted pastor and a fine choir. Sunday school starts at 9:30. Worship is at 11:00."

"Thanks," Hildy said. "I'll tell the others."

As the girls walked back down the road, Ruby whispered, "Ain't he jist about the nicest man ye ever did meet?"

"He's sure being nice to all of us. Well, let's go see if we can find my father."

"Air ye a-gonna tell me why ye was askin' Mr. Cowan all them questions?" Ruby asked as the girls walked side by side toward town.

"I'm not really sure," Hildy said evasively. "I'm just trying to figure some things out."

"Lemme he'p ye. Ye was figgerin' thar was gold bars in them sacks ye seen Trey Granger a-carryin'. An' we both seen Garrett Kayne with a sack he was a-gonna leave at that white house when he spotted us an' took out after us. Ye figger thar was a stolen gold bar in each sack, don't ye?"

"That's part of it."

Ruby exploded in exasperation. "What d'ye mean, *part* of it? Why, it's plain as the nose on yore face what's a-goin' on! If each of them left one bar worth nearly $40,000 apiece, whoever's a-livin' in that white house woulda got nearly one hundred thousand dollars in a couple o' nights! So what other part do ye need—'ceptin' who lives in that house?"

"You're forgetting that those prices are based on what the government pays for gold. But if you multiply a stolen 89-pound gold bar by the $700 an ounce it's worth on the world market—"

"Wait! Lemme figger it out!" Ruby began figuring in the air again with her finger. "Twelve ounces times $700 is . . . $8,400 a pound—troy, that is. That, times 89 pounds is—" She scribbled frantically in the air, then shook her head. "I cain't git it!"

"It's $747,600 a gold bar, if I figured it correctly," Hildy said. "About three-quarters of a million dollars each!"

Ruby whistled in amazement, then frowned. "No wonder there's been killin's over sich things! Say, ye reckon maybe Jack's father knew who was highgrading an' they done him in to keep him from talkin'?"

"Maybe. Anybody stealing gold worth that kind of money might be desperate enough to do anything, including hurting us."

The girls arrived at the two-story wooden depot with its attached one-story side rooms that spread out on either side like outstretched wings. The depot was quiet. The man behind the ticket window said Joe Corrigan still hadn't returned and he didn't know when to expect him.

Hildy murmured her thanks and walked outside with her cousin. They stood on the high platform looking toward the shiny narrow-gauge rails. An engine and tender moved by with bell clanging, while puffs of smoke and a hiss of white steam shot out over the driver wheels.

"Now what?" Ruby asked as the noon whistle blew from one of the distant mines.

"I guess we'd better get some lunch. Maybe Daddy will be here when we get back."

The cousins jumped off the rough wooden loading platform, crossed the paved area to the first set of tracks, and headed uphill toward town.

They walked in thoughtful silence until Ruby broke it. "Think out loud."

"I don't know where to start. My mind's going like crazy. I

was wondering how I could get that washing machine for Molly, and if we'll solve this case so Mr. Farnham can have the money to build a hospital so people like Gladys Cassell won't die.

"And I was thinking about Jack's father and time running out, and who owns that house where those men left those sacks, and what Brother Ben learned at the police station, and how close I came to fall—" Hildy let her words trail off. "Look! There's Brother Ben! Come on, let's go see what he found out."

The big yellow Packard whipped sharply to the curb. The old ranger leaned across the front seat and opened the passenger door. "Get in, quick! I've got news."

Ruby muttered, "From the sound of his voice, it ain't good!"

CHAPTER Fourteen

TWISTS AND TURNS

Friday Afternoon

With Hildy sitting in the middle and Ruby in the right-front passenger seat, the old ranger turned the Packard away from the curb.

Hildy looked up at him. "What kind of news do you have?" she asked.

"I found out who lives in that white house on Hardluck Hill."

"Who is it?" Hildy asked eagerly.

"Garrett Kayne."

"I mighta knowed!" Ruby exclaimed. "He's the one that found Jack's father after he got kilt. An' he had a fight with Jack's father jist afore that too. Now he's done got his ol' job back as shift boss at the mine."

Hildy scowled, thinking fast. "I don't understand. If Garrett Kayne lives there, why did he park in front the other night instead of going back to his garage?"

Ben Strong smiled. "I asked my police contacts the same thing. They said there is no garage. Used to be, but it burned down about a year ago."

"Now we know for shore he's one of them highgraders!"

Ruby blurted. "So when kin he be arrested?"

"Not so fast! We don't have any proof that would hold up in a court of law. A man certainly has a right to carry things into his own house. And Hildy, you saw Trey Granger carrying another sack before that, but you didn't see it delivered to Kayne's—"

"We know what was in that sack!" Ruby broke in. "Gold!"

"I suspect as much," the old man commented, slowing to cross the railroad tracks, "but exactly why did Granger deliver a sack of it to Kayne's house?"

" 'Cause he's greedy, that's why!" Ruby explained. "Me'n Hildy jist talked to Mr. Cowan, an' he tol' us them gold bars weighs 89 pounds each, so at the U.S. gove'ment price, that comes to $37,380 each!"

As the tires bounced across the tracks, Ben glanced over at Ruby. "Is that a fact?"

"Shore is. Ain't that right, Hildy?"

"That's what Mr. Cowan said, but I just thought of something that doesn't make sense. Ruby, you remember seeing Garrett Kayne carry that white sack from his car?"

"Reckon I won't never forget!"

"Did he seem to be struggling as though he was carrying something very heavy?"

Ruby hesitated. "Not egg-zactly, now that ye mention it. Leastwise, not somethin' weighin' 89 pounds."

"That's what I was thinking. Neither was Trey Granger having any trouble carrying the white sack the night before."

The old ranger mused, "So whatever those men were carrying, it wasn't a gold ingot. Is that what you're thinking?"

The cousins exchanged glances before Hildy nodded. "I think there was gold in those sacks, but not a gold bar." She paused, then shook her head. "I thought we were about to solve this case, but now I'm not so sure."

"We have to ask some more questions," Ben Strong said. "But we're making progress."

"Not fast enough," Hildy said. Then she explained about the

adventure with the second shaft.

They were nearing the train depot when Hildy finished. The old ranger suddenly whipped the car off into a graveled parking lot and turned around.

"Where you going?" Hildy asked anxiously, glancing toward the depot where she hoped to see her father.

"To see if we can stop young Jack Tremayne from making those ladder repairs!" He accelerated the car so fast the tires threw gravel behind it. "If he's right about his father, it would be better if some law-enforcement men went down into the mine with him to see the evidence he claims to have."

The old ranger explained that because the mine was in the county, he would ask the sheriff's department to send some deputies along with Jack. The deputies would have to be familiar with mines. They would probably also know who the powder monkey was and could ask him to hold off blasting the mine shut until the investigation was completed.

"That way," Ben concluded in his soft drawl, "nobody outside the law-enforcement community and us will know about this."

Hildy said, "Sounds good, Brother Ben."

"There's just one problem," he added thoughtfully as he headed the Packard out of the city limits toward the mine. "I just hope there's nobody in the sheriff's department who's loose-tongued."

Ruby repeated, "Loose-tongued?"

"Yes. Although I have the greatest respect for lawmen, there's so much money involved that it's possible Garrett Kayne has a contact inside the law-enforcement community who could be bribed to pass along confidential information to him. But it's a risk we have to take."

They caught up with Jack Tremayne just past the hobo jungle along the railroad tracks. He was carrying a clawhammer and a Prince Albert tobacco can filled with nails. He turned around as the car stopped, and Hildy introduced the boy to the old ranger.

Jack looked at the girls suspiciously. "What's going on? Did you two decide to try stopping me?"

Ruby stuck her head out of the car. "Brother Ben says if'n ye'll wait, maybe he kin git some men to he'p ye."

"There's no time! I told you that. They're going to blow up this shaft by tomorrow, and then it'll be too late."

"Don't be so all-fahred pig-haided!" Ruby exploded. "I declare, yo're a-gittin' as bad as Spud!"

Hildy leaned across Ruby to speak to Jack. "Brother Ben says he thinks he can get the sheriff's office to find the powder monkey and get him to hold off on the blasting for a few days, at least long enough to have some men go in with you to see the evidence you say will show what really happened to your father."

The boy considered her words for a moment. "It sure would be better if some lawmen could see what's down there. Then they'd have the evidence needed to make an arrest. I just hope nothing happens to it in the meantime."

Hildy sighed with relief and told Jack to hop in. As Jack climbed reluctantly into the back seat, Hildy desperately hoped the old ranger's idea worked, because if it didn't, she was still committed to securing the rope while Ruby, Spud, and Jack went down into the mine.

They were headed back to town before Hildy realized that Ben was gently questioning Jack about why he was so sure his father's death was no accident.

Jack was evasive. "You'll have to see it for yourself, Mr. Strong."

Hildy tried to picture the eighty-six-year-old man trying to climb down the rickety ladder. "Oh!" she exclaimed, thinking of a way to save him such a feat. "Brother Ben will stay up on top and see that nobody disturbs you while you're showing the deputies what you found."

The old ranger gave his walrus moustache a flip with the back of his right forefinger and smiled at Hildy in appreciation. "I'd welcome some company too. How about you girls staying up there with me?"

"I kin do anythin' any boy kin do, includin' Jack—an' 'specially Spud!" Ruby declared. "Hildy, ye kin stay on top, but me, I'm a-gonna go in with them dep'ties!"

Hildy swallowed hard, embarrassed about her claustrophobia. Her fear was something she couldn't explain, so she didn't try. Instead, she changed the subject. "Jack, where'd Spud go when you two got back to town after we went down the mine shaft?"

"He said something about going to talk to Skeezix."

Jack leaned forward and rested his elbows on the back of the front seat. "I think he believes everything that old character tells him."

Hildy asked, "You think Skeezix would lie?"

Jack shrugged. "Every kid in town knows he's off his trolley. Always talking about the good old days when he was on the railroad. He tells some wild stories."

Hildy squirmed, feeling uncomfortable at anything unkind said about the retired railroad man. He'd saved her from Trey Granger and Garrett Kayne, and had helped her uncle Nate get away from the two men who'd beat up on him. Most of all, Hildy liked the old man, and thought he was able to keep a secret. After all, he'd refused to tell her certain things.

She was reluctant to hear Jack say more, but she had to know what he was thinking, so she asked, "What kind of wild stories?"

"Oh, about wrecks the narrow-gauge railroad has had, fires, runaway cars in the hills—things like that."

Hildy took a slow breath, feeling better, but Ruby spoiled her sense of relief.

"He never tol' ye nothin' about no gold train?" she asked Jack.

"Oh, that!" the boy's voice showed his disbelief. "Skeezix always thinks he knows when the railroad's getting ready to haul gold from the mines to Colfax. But, like I said, he's off his trolley."

"You mean you don't believe him?"

"Would you? Can you imagine how many desperate men there are out there who'd snatch the chance to rob that train if they knew when it was going to run? One gold bar would make them rich. And a whole trainload—why, whoever got away with that much gold could live like a king!" Jack leaned back in the rear seat and laced his fingers behind his head. "A king!"

Hildy couldn't turn to look at Jack. She felt foolish, believing the old man's hints that a trainload of gold was being readied for shipment.

Ruby leaned close and whispered, "Ye reckon he's plumb right about ol' Skeezix?"

Hildy shrugged, feeling uncomfortable.

Ben Strong finally spoke in his soft drawl, "I don't know about this Skeezix, but the law-enforcement people tell me they've picked up a rumor that there's going to be an attempt robbery of that train."

Hildy smiled her appreciation of the old ranger's coming to her rescue.

"That's nothing new!" Jack said. "Why, rumors go around several times a year that somebody's going to highjack the gold train. But nothing ever comes of it."

With that, the conversation ended. Jack got out at the depot with his hammer and can of nails to walk home. Hildy glanced around for Skeezix, but he was nowhere in sight.

Hildy's father was just coming off work, so he got in the car for the short ride back to Mrs. Callahan's Room and Board. Hildy questioned him about where he'd been working, but he smiled and said he couldn't talk about it.

Ruby whispered in Hildy's ear, "Bet he was a-workin' on that thar gold train, an' Skeezix was tellin' us the gospel truth. Ye know, I think Jack's no better'n old Spud. Boys! They shore air a pain!"

Hildy was glad Brother Ben was with them when she and Ruby told her father about their experience in the second mine shaft, because he became very upset. The old ranger saved her from the severe scolding she would surely have received. Even though Ben didn't say anything, his very presence saved her.

She had another reprieve when she saw Ruby's father walking along the street with his Cousin Jack lunch pail. "Look!" Hildy exclaimed, pointing in his direction. "There's Uncle Nate!"

Ruby leaned forward. "I been a-wonderin' how he made out today, after them two mean men hurt him so bad las' night."

"Let's find out," Ben said, pulling up alongside the tall, slender man.

Nate Konning turned around and almost ran to the curb. He stooped to look into the car. "Hi, everyone. You can't possibly guess what happened today!"

"We give up," Ruby said quickly. "What happened?"

Her father lowered his voice. "I think we're about to solve the mystery of the vanishing gold!"

Chapter Fifteen

HOPE RISES, THEN FADES

Late Friday Afternoon and Early Evening

What do you mean, we're about to solve the mystery of the vanishing gold?" Hildy exclaimed.

Her uncle reached for the door handle. "Wait'll I crawl in the back seat with Joe, and I'll tell you while we're driving. We sure don't want anyone to overhear."

Hildy and Ruby leaned forward in the front seat to let Nate Konning slide into the back. He settled his Cornish miner's lunch pail between his feet to keep it from falling over.

"Hurry up, Daddy!" Ruby cried impatiently. "Tell us what ye mean."

Her father grinned at her. "Remember I told you I asked the Lord to prepare some miner's heart so I could witness to him? Well, guess who that person was? Trey Granger!"

Hildy blinked in surprise and heard Ruby suck in her breath. Hildy asked, "The man Spud and I saw in Lone River with the stolen gold, and I saw carrying—?"

"The same!" her uncle assured her. "I'd noticed yesterday

that he seemed to have something on his mind. So today I sat alone in a stope to eat, praying he'd come. Sure enough, he did!"

From the driver's seat the old ranger asked quietly, "What did he say?"

"Well, when I was making my rounds as tool nipper first thing this morning, I noticed that Trey seemed really surprised to see me.

"Then I saw he was looking at the bruises on my face, and the way I walked—sort of stiff because of the pain in my ribs where those men beat up on me last night. Well, I can't describe the look on his face exactly, but it was sort of like he was both glad and sorry.

"He didn't say anything to me, but I had a hunch he wanted to talk to me, private-like. So at lunch, when I was eating alone in that stope, Trey came up to me. At first, he was sort of nervous, looking around and talking low. So I tried to encourage him, asking how he was doing and such. Finally he opened up."

"Daddy, please!" Ruby complained. "What'd he say?"

"He said, 'I need to talk to someone real bad, and I heard you were a part-time preacher, so I wondered if I could talk to you?' So I said, 'Sure!' and invited him to sit down by me."

"Then what happened, Daddy?" Ruby asked.

"He said he knew a man who had a chance to do something that would make him a lot of money, which he desperately needed. He knew it was wrong, but it didn't seem like it was a really bad thing at the time, so he did it."

"He was a-talkin' about hisself he'pin' to highgrade gold?" Ruby guessed.

"I'm sure of it," her father answered. "Anyway, Trey then told me something went wrong for his 'friend,' and something terrible happened; but that his friend didn't have anything to do with it, though he's afraid he'll be blamed anyway."

"Ye think he meant what happened to Jack's daddy?" Ruby asked.

Her father nodded. "I think that's what he meant, but he

didn't say, and I didn't push him. Instead, I talked to him about what the Bible says. That got to him, and tears started running down his cheeks. I started to ask if I could pray for him, but he suddenly jumped up.

"He said under his breath, 'I see the shift boss comin', but I'd like to talk to you some more tomorrow.' Then he left real fast. A minute later, Garrett Kayne walked by where I was sitting."

"You think he saw you and Trey talking?" Ben asked.

"I'm sure he did."

Hildy asked, "So that's what you meant about thinking this case is about to be solved? You think Trey's going to tell you about what happened to Jack's father?"

"I wouldn't be surprised," her uncle replied. "Trey was so upset I think he might have told me the whole truth right then if Garrett hadn't come along."

The old ranger said, "If what Jack said about his father is true, and Trey knows that Garrett Kayne is responsible, Kayne might decide he can't risk letting Trey talk to you again."

Hildy felt a cold chill sweep over her. "You think Mr. Kayne would—?"

"I'd better try to get some protection for Trey," Ben interrupted. "For you, too, Nate."

"Me?" Ruby's father asked.

"Yes, you. Suppose Garrett Kayne is guilty, and he thinks Trey has already told you the whole story? Kayne might feel he can't take any chances with either of you."

Nate said quietly, "I hadn't thought of it that way. They've been trying to scare us off."

"Yes, and I'm afraid it'll go beyond trying to scare us off," Ben warned. "Everyone of us is in some jeopardy until we solve this case. As soon as I drop all of you off at your accommodations, I'll pick up Spud and go talk to my lawman contacts. Tonight at our regular meeting place I'll tell all of you what kind of protection they can give us, including Trey Granger."

Darkness had fallen when Hildy and her father arrived at

the secluded grove of ponderosas outside of town. Hildy was anxious because of the increased threat to all of them, especially to Ruby's father and Trey Granger.

The old ranger opened the meeting. "By now, we're all aware of what happened to everyone else during the day."

Hildy's father replied, "The only thing we don't know is what you found out after you dropped us off this afternoon."

Ben continued, "The police department will try to keep all of us under surveillance while we're in town, because that's their jurisdiction. They'll especially look out for you, Nate, and Trey Granger. The mine is in the county, where sheriff's deputies patrol, so they'll keep an eye on both you men while you're above ground. But they can't protect either of you in the mines."

Hildy protested, "But that's where it'd be more dangerous for Uncle Nate and Trey Granger!"

"That's true," the old ranger agreed, "but I can understand that deputies can't be everywhere."

Hildy's father asked, "What about sending officers with Jack to check out his story?"

"The sheriff said he'd send deputies to do that tomorrow morning. I'll remind them to bring ropes in case they decide to go down through the Bighill shaft."

"What about the powder monkey?" Hildy asked. "Did the officers find him?"

"No, he's apparently working the night shift. His wife said he'd already gone to work when the officers showed up at his house this evening."

Hildy scowled, her thoughts jumping. "What happens if he decides to blow up that second shaft before he goes home tomorrow morning? That's the last day he has to do it, according to what Jack said."

"I know," Ben said soberly. "It's a risk we have to take, because there's no way of getting word to the powder monkey until after he gets off work."

Hildy continued her protest, "But if he does blow up the other shaft, there's no way Jack can prove what he says happened to his father."

Ruby turned to her father. "Reckon ye could go down in the mine tonight, find this here powder monkey, an' tell him to hold off with the dynamite?"

Nate Konning shook his head. "No, because it's not my shift, and they wouldn't let me in. You wouldn't believe what everyone goes through each day to insure that gold isn't being stolen.

"When we get to work, we all go into a big room and change out of our regular clothes. Buck naked, we walk across to where we put on mining clothes, shoes, and hat. When we come back at night, we hand our lunch buckets to the security men.

"They check those while we're stripping to the skin again and getting into our regulars, or what the Cornishmen call 'come-to-ee and go-forth-ee' clothes. We're given our lunch buckets back on the way out."

"Yet millions of dollars in gold is highgraded," Ben observed, "but it's all done quietly. Nobody dares talk about it because, as they say, 'Highgrading means silence—or death.' "

Hildy shivered, glancing around nervously and wondering if somebody were hiding in the shadows of the surrounding ponderosas, watching and listening.

Ruby spoke up. "Couldn't y'all jist have Garrett Kayne arrested an' hope this Mr. Granger'll confess later so's ye could keep the man in jail?"

Ben Strong shook his head. "There's no evidence for an arrest. Besides, catching one man won't stop the highgrading."

"That's right," Hildy's father agreed. "There's got to be several people involved, and we need to catch them all to keep Matt Farnham from being robbed blind."

Ruby exclaimed, "But we already know who they be! There's Garrett Kayne. He's boss of the highgraders. An' Jack said his father had fired Kayne—we don't know why—and then Kayne got into a fist fight with Jack's father jist a-fore he got kilt. And then Kayne was the last person to see Jack's father alive, 'cause right after that, the old sweaty dynamite blew up and caved in part of the mine on him.

"Now Mr. Kayne has Jack's father's old job so he kin steal all he wants 'cause he's now the shift boss. As fer Trey Granger, why, he all but tol' muh daddy he's in on the highgradin', and from the way he acted, he was probably in on what happened to Jack's father too."

"I don't think so, honey," Ruby's father said. "I have a hunch he started out helping with the highgrading, but something went wrong—like the death of Jack's father—and now Trey's afraid he's in a whole lot more trouble than he planned for."

Ruby defended herself. "Maybe so, but at least we know for shore that he's the one Hildy and Spud saw in Lone River with some gold that Mr. Farnham reco'nized as comin' from his mine up here. So he's a highgrader."

Spud asked, "What about the man who drove the car Hildy and I saw Trey Granger get into back in Lone River?"

"That's Casper Cobb," Ruby answered. "Have him arrested too."

"On what charges?" Spud asked, his tone a little tart. "Just because Hildy and I saw him with Trey Granger doesn't necessarily mean he knew about the gold Trey was carrying."

"Ye make me so dadblamed mad!" Ruby cried, turning toward the boy. "Don't ye see? When Trey confesses to muh daddy, Trey'll tell how Casper Cobb was in on the whole thing! What more do ye need?"

"Whoa, there!" Ruby's father said, reaching out to touch her arm. "We don't know that Trey will confess any such thing to me. Remember, in this country, everybody has to be figured innocent until proven guilty. Isn't that right, Brother Ben?"

"Right as rain," the old ranger said quietly. "Whether or not all those men are involved in the highgrading, we have to consider Jack's claim. If he's right about his father, the person or persons responsible must also be brought to justice. And one more thing: there may be others in this gang of highgraders."

"Such as?" Hildy prompted.

"Well, there's probably a fence. I've learned that Oakland, across from San Francisco, has some highgrade fences. So does Reno, Nevada, across the Sierras."

Spud chimed in. "Don't forget that truck driver and his friend who ran Hildy, Ruby, and Spud away from the place where the mine dumped waste rock."

"That's right," Nate Konning agreed. "They're the same ones who beat up on me. So they're in on this highgrading too."

"Maybe there's at least one other person," the old ranger said. "Somebody's got to transport the highgraded gold from here to wherever it's sold to a fence or taken to Mexico to get the world price."

Ruby shook her head in dismay. "I never figgered it was so all-fahred mixed up! How kin we'uns ever ketch all them people in the little bit o' time we got left?"

Hildy nodded, feeling discouragement begin to steal over her mind and body. Then an idea hit her. "Why couldn't we find where Trey Granger lives and go see him tonight? Uncle Nate, maybe he'd tell you everything. Then there'd be enough evidence for Mr. Kayne to be arrested. And everybody'd be safe!"

She watched eagerly as the three men discussed that possibility. They didn't know where Trey lived, but Ben said he could find out from his law-enforcement contacts.

Ben finally nodded. "It's worth a try. But if Trey won't talk to you, Nate, we know the police will be watching over him tonight. Tomorrow in the mine, your job as tool nipper will allow you to move around, so you can look out for Trey."

"Who's a-gonna look out after muh daddy down thar in that ol' mine?" Ruby asked.

"I'll be fine, honey," her father assured her.

As everyone started to leave, Hildy thought of something else. "How about Jack? Shouldn't we go by his place tonight and tell him what's going on? I mean, suppose he goes out there to the second shaft early tomorrow morning and the place gets blown up while he's down in the mine?"

"He said he'd wait fer us," Ruby said.

"Yes, he said he'd wait to go down in the mine, but not to fix the ladder. Remember? We picked him up this afternoon before he got there with his hammer and nails."

Ben said soberly, "It sounds like a good idea to at least go by his home and alert him to what could happen. You girls know where he lives?"

Hildy and Ruby shook their heads.

"That's okay," he said. "We can find out from the same source that'll tell us where Trey lives. Hildy, I'm sure you'd like to be the one to tell Jack, so I'll take you to his house right after we check with the police."

About forty-five minutes later, Ben pulled the Packard away from the police station and stopped in front of a small frame house on the outskirts of Quartz Hill. There were no street-lamps, so when the old ranger turned off his headlights, deep darkness settled over everything.

Ben switched the lights on again. "You'll need them to see by," he said. "You want someone to go with you?"

Hildy shook her head, slid out of the car, and walked rapidly up the dirt path and onto the small porch. As soon as she knocked, the door opened. A middle-aged woman stood inside the screen door. She flipped on the outside porch light, then wiped her hands on an apron. A couple of little girls peered from behind the woman's frayed housedress.

"Oh," the woman said, her heavily lined face looking sad, "I thought you was Jack, and he forgot his key."

A sense of uneasiness suddenly gripped Hildy. "He's not home?"

"No." The woman shook her head. "I'm Jack's mother, and I'm worried. You see, a man came by about two hours ago with a message from a new friend of Jack's—named Hildy."

"I'm Hildy. But I didn't send any message."

Mrs. Tremayne dropped her apron and her hands flew to her mouth in alarm. "You didn't?"

"No." Hildy paused, seeing the woman's face tighten in fear. "Uh . . . who was this man? What was the message?"

"Oh, my stars!" the woman cried. "Something terrible's happened to my boy!"

CHAPTER
SIXTEEN

———

RACING AGAINST
THE CLOCK

Friday Night

H ildy fought back her own fear and spoke through the
screen door. "Please, Mrs. Tremayne! Tell me, who was
the man?"

"I never saw him before."

"What'd he look like?"

"Oh, he was about six feet tall, in his early twenties. Had a
long, skinny face and a blond moustache."

Trey Granger! Hildy thought. That made her feel a little better.
Aloud, she repeated, "What was the message?"

"What?" Jack's mother was still stunned at the news that
Hildy hadn't sent any message.

"Like, where Jack was to meet . . . uh . . . me?"

"I don't remember. Oh yes, I do. The man said he'd take
Jack to meet you . . . her."

"Anything else you can remember?" Hildy asked.

"I don't think so. But what's this all about? What's happened
to my boy?"

"I'll try to find out," Hildy promised, turning away toward the car's headlights. "Then I'll let you know."

Hildy got back in the front seat of the car as Ben started the motor. She looked back at Jack's mother and little sisters. They had come out onto the small porch and stood there uncertainly. Hildy ached for them.

She forced her eyes away from the sad sight and quickly reported what Jack's mother had said.

Ruby asked, "Why do ye reckon Trey went and done sich a thing as that?"

Hildy shrugged. "I don't know."

The old ranger suggested, "Since we'll be going to Trey's house so Nate can talk to him, why don't we just ask Trey what this is all about?"

"Yeah!" Ruby agreed. "I betcha that's whar Jack is this very instant."

The Packard picked up speed as Ben drove toward the area where his contacts had told him Trey lived. Hildy looked thoughtfully through the windshield, watching the car's big headlights bounce along a quiet Quartz Hill back street.

Hildy said, "I'm trying to figure out why Trey mentioned me to Jack's mother. How'd Trey know my name?"

"He shore should know about ye!" Ruby said. "He done seen you an' Spud a-follerin' him in Lone River. Then him an' that other feller chased ye through Quartz City the night ol' Skeezix saved ye. So why shouldn't Trey tell Jack's mother ye wanted to see him?"

"But that doesn't explain how Trey knew my name. And how did he know Jack would come with him when he said I'd sent a message that I wanted to see Jack?"

"Let's hope Trey's home," Hildy's father said, "and we'll find out. Nate, since he's confided in you, maybe you should go in alone."

Nate agreed, so when Ben stopped the Packard outside a long frame house with the porch light on, Ruby's father walked up to the door and knocked. Moments later a young, dark-haired woman opened the door. Hildy vainly strained to hear what was said through the screen door.

Hildy's uncle turned back to the car. The front door closed on the house. The porch light went out.

"Well?" Hildy asked as Nate Konning got back into the car.

"That was Trey's wife. She said he took a kid someplace so they could talk. Mrs. Granger didn't seem to know what it was about or where they went. I could see she was a little concerned, because she said Trey has been very upset lately. She said she didn't know why, but thought it had something to do with his new job."

Hildy asked, "How long has he worked at the mine?"

"His wife said just a few months. Before that he'd been a pilot at an airport near Oakland, but he couldn't make enough money flying, so he went to work at the Shasta Daisy."

"Did his wife give you any idea where he and Jack might have gone?" Hildy asked.

"No, but she said that when her husband wants to think, he sometimes gets in his car and drives around. He likes to watch the trains, so he often parks near the depot. How about we look there?"

Everyone agreed, so the old ranger headed the car toward the depot. As they drove, Hildy's mind returned to the nagging question: *How did Trey know my name?*

Except for those with whom she'd ridden up from Lone River, only four people knew her name. *Mrs. Callahan, Jack Tremayne, Skeezix, and Leith Cowan. So one of them had to have told Trey my name. But which one? And why?*

After a moment's reflection, Hildy had the answer to her last question. Trey would have wanted to know her name because she and Spud had followed him in Lone River. He had chased her with Casper Cobb the night Skeezix had saved her from their pursuit.

Ruby broke into Hildy's thoughts. "Ye reckon that's the gold train Skeezix was a-tellin' us about?"

Hildy focused her eyes on the small but powerful narrow-gauge steam engine. There were two short blasts on the whistle, and it started pulling away from the station with bell clanging and black smoke pouring out of the stack.

"I have no idea," Hildy replied. "Skeezix didn't tell us how they make up the train when it's taking a shipment of gold ingots to Colfax."

"If it air a gold train," Ruby said thoughtfully, "do ye reckon whoever's been highgradin' from Mr. Farnham's mine has any of his stolen gold on that thar train?"

Hildy started to shrug, then blinked and sat upright as a thought struck her. "Uncle Nate, did Mrs. Granger say Trey had been a pilot?"

"Yes. Why?"

"Wouldn't the fastest way to get stolen gold from here to Mexico be by airplane?"

Her uncle replied, "Yes, I suppose so. But I don't know if one could fly that far."

The old ranger said, "Yes, aircraft can easily do that. Gold's very heavy, but with the price at $700 an ounce on the world market, one private monoplane could easily carry a fortune right out of the Quartz City airport. Hildy, your idea strikes me as being so logical that I'll check it out with my law-enforcement contacts before we have to leave tomorrow."

Tomorrow! Hildy's mind jumped. *That's all the time we've got left to solve this case. If we don't, there'll be no washing machine for Molly and no hospital for Lone River.*

"There!" she suddenly exclaimed, pointing through the windshield. "I think that's Trey's car. See it? Parked at the far end of the depot."

Hildy saw Trey's startled face when the Packard's headlights struck his car. She also got a glimpse of Jack sitting beside the driver. Trey made furtive movements as though he was about to start the car.

"He's going to run away!" Nate Konning shouted. "Brother Ben, stop the car! Girls, let me squeeze past you. Hurry!"

Trey's car began to vibrate with life as Hildy's uncle ran up to the driver's side window. "Trey, it's me, Nate Konning. We need to talk."

Hildy watched with concern as the tall young man slowly relaxed.

Ruby's father turned around to face the Packard. "Would you folks give us a few minutes alone, please?"

Ben shifted into low gear and pulled the Packard down to the opposite end of the depot but where Trey's car was still visible. Hildy caught a glimpse of her uncle as he settled in the passenger's seat with Jack between him and the driver.

The old ranger turned off the motor and lights, and darkness engulfed everyone inside.

Ruby asked quietly, "Ye reckon Trey done tol' Jack about bein' a highgrader, but claimin' he didn't know nothin' about plans fer Jack's father bein' kilt?"

"We'll soon find out," Hildy answered, letting her eyes roam along the railroad tracks. She wondered briefly where Skeezix was, then turned to look toward Trey's car.

"I wish I'd thought to have Uncle Nate ask Trey how he knew my name," Hildy said. "That's a question that really bothers me."

Time seemed to drag as they waited in the Packard for Nate to return. The night cold seeped into the car, chilling Hildy's legs. She tried not to think about her discomfort by letting her mind wander over the various concerns pressing in all around. Names and faces whirled in and out of her thoughts. *Casper Cobb. Garrett Kayne. The red-faced truck driver and his burly helper. Leith Cowan. Mrs. Callahan.*

A narrow-gauge locomotive came out of the night, its single headlight piercing the darkness ahead and making the twin rails glisten with a silver sheen. By now everyone's breath in the Packard had fogged up the car windows.

"Whatcha thinkin', Hildy?" Ruby asked quietly.

"Oh, lots of things. But mostly I was trying to figure this thing out because tomorrow's our deadline for solving this case."

"There ain't much time left," Ruby admitted.

"So unless something happens real fast, Mr. Farnham's gold

is going to continue to be stolen, and that means there won't be a hospital in Lone River. And we won't know the truth about Jack's father."

"Maybe Trey's confessin' to muh daddy this very instant, and then we kin git those crooks arrested so we kin all go home happy."

"Guess we'll know in a minute," Hildy said, looking out the steamed-up window. "Uncle Nate's coming back."

Hildy opened the door to let him in. "What did he say?" she asked impatiently. "And what about Jack?"

"Trey said his little talk with me at lunch today gave him the courage to make a decision."

"About what?" Hildy asked as Ben started the motor and turned toward the street.

"He said he decided to tell Jack first about the highgrading and then the truth of what happened to his father. But Trey wasn't sure Jack would go with him, so he used Hildy's name. Then he took the boy out here where they could talk.

"Trey confessed to Jack and to me that he's part of the gang that's been stealing millions of dollars worth of gold from Matt Farnham's mine."

"So now we know for the first time that Trey's telling the truth," Ben said, easing the Packard across railroad tracks. "But who are the others in the gang?"

"Besides Trey, there's Garrett Kayne, Casper Cobb, and someone called Rasor. He's the truck driver who ran you kids off and beat up on me with the help of his swamper. I didn't get his full name."

"Who's the ringleader?" Ben asked.

"I forgot to ask!" Hildy's uncle shook his head in self-reproach. "But I'd guess it's Kayne."

"Go on," Hildy urged. "What else did Trey tell you?"

"He told me what he'd already told Jack—that Jack's father found out about the highgrading and said he wouldn't have it on his shift. He told them that if they didn't stop, he'd tell Matthew Farnham. Jack's father died shortly after that."

"So Jack's father threatened to tell the banker, and ended up dead," Ben said in his soft drawl.

"How awful!" Hildy exclaimed.

"But Trey claims he didn't know that was going to happen," Hildy's uncle continued. "And he didn't want to be involved any more. Yet he didn't dare say anything about wanting out, because he's afraid for his own life."

"Will he testify to all this?" the old ranger asked.

"Better than that," Nate answered. "When he heard what Jack had to say about his father's death and his plans to go into the mine tomorrow to show others, Trey decided to play along."

Ruby asked, "How's that?"

Her father explained. "Trey said he was hired as an electrician, although he really doesn't know much about that trade. But it's one of the few jobs that gives a workman free run of the mines, which is what he needed to help in the highgrading, and he is never searched.

"Anyway, when I told them about the deputies meeting Jack tomorrow so he can show them the evidence, we agreed on a plan."

"What kind of plan?" Hildy asked.

"Tomorrow morning Trey will go down the Shasta Daisy to work as usual. Then he'll go through the passages to where Jack's father died. Jack will accompany the deputies down through the second shaft and along the connecting passageway to meet Trey. Nobody'll know they're there."

Ben concluded with his own assumption: "Then Trey will give the officers his statement, naming his accomplices. He'll try to prove to the deputies that these accomplices caused the dynamite to go off on purpose, but that Trey knew nothing of it until it was too late. Right?"

"That's about the size of it," Ruby's father said. "Now all we have to do is pray that everything goes according to plan. If it does, the case of the highgraded gold is not only solved for Matt Farnham, but justice will be done for Jack's father."

Spud said grimly, "I remember hearing that nobody's ever

been convicted in court for highgrading gold. Let's just hope
there will be a conviction for murder."

Ben drove by Mrs. Tremayne's house, where Hildy reported
that Jack was all right and would soon be home. As the Packard
headed back to town, Hildy leaned back against the front seat
and closed her eyes.

What had looked more and more hopeless and confusing
earlier today now seemed to be filled with hope and certainty,
yet Hildy had a vague sense of fear.

She voiced her thoughts. "When Trey confesses to the police,
and Jack shows them the evidence he's found, Garrett Kayne
and Casper Cobb will go to jail.

"But what about Trey? I know he's guilty of helping steal
gold, but at least he wasn't involved in what happened to Jack's
father."

"Trey will probably turn state's evidence," the old ranger explained. "He may get some jail time, but certainly not as much
as the ones involved in the murder."

"If all goes well," Hildy said, "and we make our deadline,
I'd like to stay over until Sunday so we can go to church with
Mr. Cowan to hear those Cornish miners in the choir. Anyway,
it sure looks as if Mr. Farnham will be able to build that hospital."

Ben Strong said quietly, "I don't know, Hildy. This seems to
be coming together too easily."

Hildy sat up and opened her eyes. "Why? What could go
wrong, Brother Ben?"

"If I knew, maybe we could stop it. But there are some loose
ends that haven't been tied up, and that means something could
go wrong."

I feel something's wrong too, Hildy admitted to herself. *Like we're
overlooking something. But what?* She shrugged it off, thinking,
It'll all be over tomorrow morning. So what could go wrong now?

She seemed to hear a small, mocking voice at the back of her
mind: *You'll find out soon enough.*

Hildy shivered, but not from the cold.

CHAPTER
SEVENTEEN

ANOTHER UNEXPECTED COMPLICATION

Early Saturday Morning

Hildy spent another restless night, disturbed by ragged thoughts. They were like loose ends of string sticking up in various directions, but she couldn't seem to tie them together. *What am I overlooking?* she asked herself repeatedly. There was no answer.

When she and her father slid into the front seat of Ben's car early the next morning, Hildy announced, "This is deadline day."

Spud spoke from the back seat, where he sat with Ruby and her father. "Yes, and we're about to wrap up the final details in the mystery of the phantom gold!"

Ben said in his quiet drawl, "I hope so."

Suddenly Hildy realized her uncle was also in the car. "I thought you were going to work in the Shasta Daisy today and keep an eye on Trey?"

Nate Konning smiled. "After Ben left us last night, he got to fretting and . . . You tell her, Ben."

"I couldn't ignore my lawman's sixth sense, so I went by Trey's house and convinced him and his wife that he should stay home today so the police could protect him."

"Now I can go with the rest of you to the second shaft," Ruby's father concluded.

"That tickles me pink," Ruby said. "I didn't cotton to the idee of him bein' down thar in that ol' mine whar somethin' turr'ble could happen to him."

The sun had not risen over the surrounding mountain ranges when the Packard stopped on the shoulder of the road near the second shaft. Hildy leaned forward anxiously, studying a dusty old Reo truck parked under a black oak tree.

"I wonder if that truck broke down?" she said, sliding out of the front seat after her father. "I'll go take a quick look."

Hildy hurried up to the driver's side of the truck, concern still gripping her from last night. There was no one around.

Hmm, Hildy mused, noticing that neither side of the hood was raised. *Whoever was driving it didn't have engine trouble.*

She glanced uneasily toward the manzanita and ponderosas that blocked the view of the mine's fallen headframe. Drawing her sweater more tightly around her, Hildy started to turn back when she stopped dead still.

She bent to study the truck's door panel. A sign was painted on it, but covered with dust so that it was impossible to make out the words. Hildy quickly began to rub the dust off as best she could with her fingers. The letters slowly emerged from the grime:

"Red Barnes," she read aloud. "EXPLOSIVES!"

She whirled toward the others who were still around the Packard. "The powder monkey!" she cried, pointing to the sign. "He must not have gotten the message last night, because he's already here!"

Hildy turned and dashed across the road toward the manzanita. "Come on!" she called. "We have to stop him before he destroys Jack's evidence!"

Not waiting for the others, she rushed past the manzanita

and ponderosas, a silent prayer on her lips.

At the shaft entrance, a powerfully built man looked up from a small bonfire. He wore high-topped leather boots, wide-flaring khaki breeches, an old sheepskin coat, and a hard hat with carbide lamp attached.

"Well, now, young lady," he said with obvious surprise. "What brings you out here so early?" His square jaw and leathery-looking face suggested he was used to a rough life.

Hildy slid to a stop, her heart thudding from the hard, short run. "What're you doing?" she demanded.

The face hardened. "I'm warming myself. Used a little dynamite to start—"

"Dynamite?" Hildy exclaimed, glancing at the fire.

"It's safe if you know what . . . More company?"

"This is my father, my uncle, my cousin, and friends. I'm Hildy Corrigan."

The three men and Spud shook hands. The stranger acknowledged the introductions with a nod. "Howdy, folks. I'm Reuben J. Barnes, but most folks call me Red. I'm the powder monkey around here. What brings all of you out here?"

Hildy tore her fascinated eyes from the fire. "Didn't the sheriff's office find you last night?"

"No, why should they find me?" the man asked.

Ben Strong briefly explained what had happened, concluding, "You apparently didn't get the message to hold off blowing this shaft shut."

"Nope, nary a word! Now, I don't mean any disrespect to you good folks, but I don't know any of you from Adam's off ox. It's not that I don't believe your story—no offense, you understand—but I have my orders to blast this thing shut today at the latest."

Hildy cried, "You mean you're going to go ahead even after what we told you?"

The powder monkey took a small, round can of snuff from his coat pocket and placed a pinch between his lower front teeth and lip. "I've had a long night down in that mine, and I'm tired and want to get home to my missus. So yes, I'm going to blast this thing shut, and I'd be obliged if all of you got back to the road."

Hildy looked imploringly at her father to see if he could suggest something to make the man change his mind. Then she glanced down and saw a red Prince Albert tobacco can lying on the ground by the hollow log.

"Those nails!" Hildy pointed to the nails that had spilled out of the flat can. "Mr. Barnes, are those yours?"

"Nope. Was here when I showed up. Why?"

Hildy's heart began to pound as she turned to look at the brush surrounding the opening to the mine shaft. "Jack's already here! He must have already gone down and repaired those rungs on the ladder!" She took a few quick steps and bent over the hollow log. "He kept his rope and lamps here. See? The rope's gone and so is one lamp." She turned toward the mine shaft.

"Look out, young lady!" Red Barnes warned. "You could fall in and be killed!"

"But Jack's down there! I'm sure of it."

Hildy peered into the darkened shaft, but saw nothing. She listened, but couldn't hear anything from the black hole half filled with debris.

The powder monkey said thoughtfully. "Well, I sure want to get this job done fast, but if somebody's down there . . . ." He paused, then added, "I'll give him a few minutes. But as soon as he pops his head out of that shaft, I'm setting my charges and blowing this place to kingdom come! Now, is that clear?"

Hildy looked at the man's hard expression and knew he meant what he said. He wasn't intimidated by two men his own age in good physical shape; that much Hildy could tell from his blunt talk.

Hildy's father said gently, "Nobody's trying to keep you from your job, sir. It's just that there's a whole lot more riding on this than we can tell you."

Barnes rubbed his chin. "You could send somebody down after him, but there's some unstable dynamite below. No sense to risk jarring it and hurt somebody."

Hildy sucked in her breath, remembering what Jack had said about the box of sweating dynamite in the mine. It could explode at a sudden noise or vibration, just as had happened when Jack's father was killed.

"We'd better wait, Red," Ben said, giving his white walrus moustache a flip with the back of his right forefinger. "By the time Jack comes back up, the deputies should be here to confirm what Hildy's told you."

Hildy wondered why Jack had repaired the ladder, brought the nails up, then apparently taken the hammer and gone back down into the mine again. Then another thought hit her: *I wonder if the dynamite will go off if Jack drops his hammer near it?*

She shook her head to drive the terrible idea away, causing her long brown braids to flop in the crisp morning air. Then she directed her focus again to the bonfire.

"Mr. Barnes—"

"Red," the man said, holding his big hands to the fire.

Hildy nodded. "Red, did you really use dynamite to start that fire?"

"Do it all the time. If you know how to handle it, dynamite's not dangerous until the cap is attached, unless it's old and unstable. Then little yellow beads form on the outside of the stick, like sweat. Very nasty stuff! Don't dare jar it."

Hildy gulped, hoping Jack wasn't close to the sweating box of dynamite below.

The powder monkey continued. "This dynamite is sawdust, soaked in a percentage of nitroglycerin and wrapped in heavy waxed paper. If you know what you're doing, you can break the stick, dump it out, and light a match to warm your hands. Of course, if you don't . . ."

He shrugged, then added, "The company gets peeved at me for doing this, but it keeps my hands warm while I get ready to blast."

Hildy looked toward the mine shaft, hoping to see Jack's head appear. She asked, "How do you go about blasting?"

"Well, keeping it as simple as I can, I place the charges where I want to blast rock loose. Then I touch it off. I used to use a slow-burning fuse. Light it with a match, yell, 'fire in the hole,' and run like mad. Now the nitro goes off from a jolt of electricity. I use a dynamite cap. That's a piece of copper tubing about the size of a pencil. It explodes with electricity, not heat.

"So I hook up two wires. Well, I connect one and keep the other away from the terminal until I'm ready to fire. I use a hotshot battery. Here, I'll show you."

"Uh, no thanks!" Hildy exclaimed, backing up.

Some time passed before Ruby said, "Wonder what's a-keepin' ol' Jack."

Ben replied, "I was wondering about that, too, and where those deputies are." He turned and looked toward the roadway.

The powder monkey glanced at the eastern sky. The sun was just topping the tips of the stately ponderosas. "Folks, I've wasted enough time—"

"You're not changing your mind, are you?" Hildy broke in, panic in her voice.

"Look at it from my viewpoint, young lady. A bunch of strangers come to me with a cockamamie story and not a shred of evidence. I've waited long enough—"

"You can't do that!"

"Oh, yes I can, young lady!" The powder monkey's gaze shifted from Hildy to the others. "Look, all of you," he began, his face flushing slightly and his voice rising. "I got my orders. I'm sleepy and tired and feeling meaner than a sow bear with cubs. Now, I tell you what. I doubt there's a kid down in that hole. So if all of you'll go on about your business, I'll go about mine."

Hildy started to protest, but her father spoke first. "Sir, I know what it's like to be dog-tired, but we're telling you there *is* a boy down in that shaft! If you don't give him time to get out—"

"Hold it right there, mister!" The powder monkey's face was grim, his cheeks turning bright red. "I don't want to hurt anybody any more'n the next man would, but I'm tired of all this chin music."

His tone changed slightly, softening a bit. "Tell you what. Someone go down in that shaft this minute and holler for that kid. If he comes out, fine. If not, I figger he's probably going out through the main shaft at the Shasta Daisy."

Hildy was aghast. "You can't be serious!"

"Dead serious, young lady! When I blow this thing up, the kid can still get out the other way. You said he's got a light. There are miners all through those drifts, and he'll hear them or they'll hear him. Now, what's it to be?"

"What if he's hurt?" Hildy protested. "Maybe that's why he's not coming back up."

Red Barnes' voice was gruff. "Every kid with half an ounce of brains knows it's dangerous to go into any mine, especially an old abandoned one like this. If he went down there alone, that's downright stupid! But I can't sit around all day, wondering about him."

"Mister," Hildy cried, "that's like saying you don't care if Jack gets killed!"

The powder monkey's voice rose. "Sure, I care! But he's not my responsibility. Blowing this thing shut *is*. Besides, I'm getting madder by the minute, and I gave you a choice. What's it going to be?"

Hildy joined the hurried discussion. Ben said quietly, "I don't think he'll really do it, but the deputies aren't here, and we've got to do something about Jack—right now."

"I'll go get him," Ruby's father volunteered. "Hildy, hand me one of those carbide lamps."

"But Uncle Nate," she sputtered, terrified at what could happen.

"It's okay, Hildy," her father said. "I'll go with him."

Panic engulfing her, Hildy blurted, "The rungs on that ladder won't hold your weight!"

Everyone looked at her.

Ruby nodded, "She's right, I reckon. Even if Jack drove more nails, them rungs is too old an' rotten for growed men."

Hildy thought of something. "The deputies. They won't be able to go down this way either."

"Maybe they'll have ropes strong enough to lower themselves," Hildy's father said. "If not, we'll think of something."

The old ranger looked toward the road, hidden by the manzanita. "Speaking of deputies, maybe they can't find this place. I'd better go see if they're lost."

"Good idea, Ben," Ruby's father replied. "If they're there, bring them back as fast as you can."

As Ben hurried toward the roadway, Hildy turned to her father and uncle. "I'm worried about Jack. He could be hurt or something."

Spud finally offered, "You men can't go, and it's no place for girls, so I'll go find Jack."

Ruby's short temper flared. "I kin do anythin' any boy kin do! I'm a-gonna go down thar with ye!"

Her father exclaimed, "Now, Ruby!"

She turned to him, eyes sparking. "Daddy, at a time like this, two haids down thar is better'n one!"

Spud said with a teasing grin, "Why Ruby, you sound as if you care what happens to me."

"That ain't got nothin' to do with it!"

"Whatever you do, get on with it," Red Barnes growled. "I'm tired of waiting."

Hildy was scared for her cousin and friend, and ashamed that they were volunteering while her claustrophobia made her hang back like a coward. She thought of her sore shoulder, thinking she could use that as an excuse not to go. But she couldn't bring herself to mention it.

"No!" Hildy exclaimed, her mouth suddenly dry from fear so that the word came out a hoarse croak. "You can't! You'll both get lost!"

"We'll follow Jack's rope and bring him up as soon as possible," Spud answered. He turned toward the fallen log and pulled out a hard hat with attached carbide lamp. "Red, you got a light for this?"

"Mine, too," Ruby said, picking up another hat.

Hildy watched in agony as the carbide gas in the two lamps hissed when flame touched the wicks. Ruby and Spud turned toward the shaft.

Spud stopped beside the yawning black hole. "Ruby, you want me to go first?"

"I reckon," she adjusted her hard hat over her short blonde hair. "Ready?"

"Ready," Spud replied, turning to step onto the first rung of the ladder.

Hildy suffered fear and then guilt as Ruby started to follow Spud. They were risking their lives, and she was standing by helplessly, letting them do it.

Hildy took a deep, shuddering breath, squared her shoulders and made a decision: "Wait!" she cried, stooping to pick up a hard hat and lamp. "I'm coming with you."

—

CHAPTER EIGHTEEN

TERROR IN THE DARK

Early Saturday Morning

Hildy borrowed Red Barnes' hard hat to replace the one she had knocked off Ruby's head in the first trip down the ladder with Jack. Her heart was thudding loudly as she shut out the protests of her father and uncle and descended the repaired ladder behind Ruby and Spud. At the bottom, she tried not to panic.

Hildy heard water dripping ominously in the darkness beyond the light of the three carbide lamps. She thought she heard the tiny squeaks of rats scurrying away. The smell of moist earth filled her nostrils, reminding her of a freshly dug grave back in the Ozarks.

But it was not these sensory impressions that bothered Hildy as much as her unreasoning fear of the small, narrow passageway in which she stood. No terror could compete with her claustrophobia.

"There's Jack's rope," she managed to say, trying desperately to quell her desire to climb back up the ladder to safety. One end was tied to the bottom rung of the ladder. From there, the rope led between two rusty ore-car tracks. Tracks and rope curved out of sight to the right.

"Jack must have played that rope out behind him as he went," Spud said, his voice making a hollow sound.

"Let's follow it," Hildy suggested. "The sooner we find him, the sooner we can get out of here."

She and Spud walked side by side inside the ore-car rails. Their lights made the blackness retreat ahead of them. The passage led upward on a steep slant.

Spud said, "I've been studying up on hardrock mining. That wide place where we stepped off the ladder is called a station. Men and supplies are delivered or taken out there. Where we are now is what the miners call a drift or a level. Remember, that's a horizontal underground passageway that follows a vein of gold. That's why we're on an uphill grade. They used steel cables to pull the cars here, but mules were used on level ground."

From behind, Ruby muttered, "Thar ye go ag'in, showin' off how smart ye think ye air!"

"Let him talk," Hildy managed to say, her heart still racing more from her claustrophobia than from walking up the incline. She tilted her head back slightly, hoping the light from her hard hat would show Jack up ahead.

They passed an underground room to the right. Hildy glanced that way, the movement making the carbide lamp on her hat shine the way she looked. There was nothing in the room except a single large boulder on the rocky floor. The boulder seemed to retreat from the light, casting huge shadows on the far wall. There were some reinforcing timbers against the low ceiling on the right.

"This is another stope, as the miners call it," Spud said as they passed. "You remember, it's an underground excavation from which the ore has been removed."

"I didn't ask ye for no word lesson!" Ruby reminded him sharply. "Let's jist find ol' Jack an' git outta here!"

They hurried on, accompanied by the unseen dripping of

water and the strange echoing sounds of their footsteps.

"Good thing this is only the first level," Spud said. "Otherwise, we'd be up to our necks in water. Pumps in some mines lift out a million gallons of water a day. That's because anything floods when it's 180 vertical feet below the ground level."

"Jist look an' don't talk!" Ruby growled.

Spud seemed not to hear. "Hildy, did you know that there are more than 300 miles of passages around here, and some are 11,000 feet below the surface?"

Ruby mimicked him under her breath. "Three hundred miles . . . 11,000 feet . . ."

Hildy was personally glad to have Spud's reassuring voice. Maybe he wasn't scared, but she was—plenty.

Spud stopped abruptly. "Listen!" he whispered urgently.

Hildy held her breath as all three stopped and stood silently.

"Hear it?" Spud asked in a stage whisper.

"Yes," Hildy replied. "It's somebody tapping."

"It's them haints!" Ruby exclaimed. "Them little whatchamacallems that Jack tol' us about."

"Tommyknockers," Spud replied.

"There aren't any such things," Hildy reassured her cousin. "That sounds like a hammer on rocks. It's probably a miner working, but I can't tell where it's coming from."

"Ain't supposed to be no miners in this here part of the mine!" Ruby muttered. Her light made quick, darting movements in all directions as she sought to locate the source of the sound. "Them's haints, and they're a-warnin' us, jist like Jack tol' us! Thar's danger down here! Let's git back fast!"

"It's stopped," Spud said softly.

Hildy listened hard. "You're right."

Ruby's voice had a slight tremor in it. "I don't keer! We been warned. Let's go back afore it's too late!"

"We can't until we find Jack," Hildy reminded her. She took a deep breath to ease the tension that made her body stiff. "Now, don't be afraid. Come on!"

Ruby mumbled, "I ain't skeered o' nothin' human, but haints ain't human!"

"Well," Spud said, "Hildy and I are going on." He turned his light back up the inclined passage.

"Ye cain't shame me, Spud!" Ruby snapped. "I kin do anything ye kin! Now, either walk fast or gitta out the way so's I kin."

Hildy smiled to herself at her feisty cousin's sudden change of mind, then led the way with Spud toward the first curve. But Hildy's heart was thudding against her ribs more than ever, and it was all she could do to keep from turning back.

They followed the tracks around the uphill curve. The three lights revealed an ore car up against the left wall where it had jumped the tracks. Part of the broken quartz and granite rocks had spilled out onto the tracks.

"That's funny," Hildy said as she drew closer. "That looks like dust still rising from where the car hit. How could that be? This car must have been here for months, at least."

Spud moved closer, focusing his light on the strange sight. "It can't have been here long," he said soberly. "That *is* dust still coming up."

"I knowed it!" Ruby whispered, her voice carrying a hint of a frightened sob. "It's them haints! They done that a-purpose."

"Not haunts," Hildy said, "or tommyknockers. Look at the cable attached to the end of the car. See how bright and shiny it is?"

Spud stooped to examine the end of the car facing uphill, away from the wall. "The cable's all rusty, but the end's bright, with no rust on it. It's been cut. And not long ago."

Hildy glanced around nervously, her light probing ahead up the dark drift. The mute tracks seemed to mock her, challenging her to figure out what had happened.

Suddenly she knew. "Somebody's in this mine besides Jack and us," she announced somberly.

"But who?" Spud asked. "And why would they have cut the cable?"

Hildy swallowed hard. "That car was meant to run Jack down. Look, isn't that his hammer up ahead, beside the tracks?"

"I see it," Spud answered. "And his rope—in fact, that's the end of his rope. But where's Jack?"

"Ye reckon the car done hit him?" Ruby asked in a hoarse whisper.

Hildy didn't answer. Still struggling against her fear, she started up the incline, shining her light on the hammer and the end of the rope. Several feet of rope lay in an untidy coil beside the tracks.

Hildy reached for the hammer, picked it up, and examined it in the light of the hissing carbide lamp. "It's Jack's all right. I'm sure of it. But where's. . . ? Look! Another stope!"

It was much smaller than the first stope they had passed. Hildy held her breath as she moved away from the tracks to examine the excavation more closely, fearful that Jack might be lying there.

"It's empty," she said. She turned back to the tracks and the coil of rope. "He must've dropped the hammer and rope when he heard the ore car coming."

Spud said, "The logical thing is that he dived out of the way of the car, which means he should be in this stope."

"So why ain't he?" Ruby asked. "Ye reckon them little haints—?"

"Ruby!" Hildy cut in a little sharply. "We're dealing with real, live people, not haunts or tommy—" She broke off her sentence as a thought hit her.

"What?" Spud asked. "What're you thinking?"

"Suppose Jack didn't have time to think about jumping in here when he heard that car coming? What would be the natural thing to do?"

"That's easy," Ruby said with an unladylike snort of derision, "Run!"

"Exactly," Hildy replied. "Run away from the sound of the approaching ore car."

"You're right," Spud agreed. "He dropped the hammer and

rope and ran back the way he came. He got past the curve where the car jumped the tracks. But if that were so, why didn't we see him?"

Hildy thought a moment. "There wasn't a cross passage, or one up or down to another level."

"A winze or raise," Spud corrected, "depending on the person's point of reference—"

"Stop it, Spud!" Ruby cut in. "Hildy, what're ye a-tryin' to say?"

"I'm saying there's only one place he could have gone—into that big stope we passed."

"That's right," Spud said. "The only other possibility is that he ran past the ladder in the shaft, and that's not logical. If he got that far, he'd have climbed out."

"If'n yo're right," Ruby said, "then why didn't we see or hear him when we passed that thar room?"

"Maybe he's hurt," Hildy guessed.

"Or," Spud added, "whoever chased him, caught him."

Ruby made a whimpering noise. "Don't say sich things!"

"We have to go back and check that first stope," Hildy insisted, leading the way back to the tracks.

She had taken only a couple of steps when she stopped. "What's that?"

Everyone stood stock-still and listened.

"Voices!" Spud whispered. "Somebody's coming!" He turned his head so the carbide lamp lit up the inclined passage. The ore car rails could be seen until they vanished into the blackness of the drift.

Ruby said hoarsely, "I don't hear nothin'! But my feet feel funny."

Hildy glanced down at her cousin's feet. Both were balanced across one narrow rail.

Spud bent quickly and laid his ear against the other rail.

"What're you doing?" Hildy asked.

"It's an old trick I learned when I was hoboing," the boy

answered, jumping up. "You can hear a train coming a long ways away."

Ruby grumbled, "They shore ain't no trains a-comin' in this here mine."

"No, but there's a car coming, and fast!" Spud snapped. "I'll bet it's another runaway."

"Quick!" Hildy exclaimed. "Back into the stope!"

Hildy, Ruby, and Spud were barely inside the excavation when another loaded ore car thundered down the incline and flashed past the opening to the stope. Seconds later, there was a crash of metal against metal and the sound of rocks falling.

"Must've jumped the tracks and hit the other car," Spud guessed.

Hildy stood still, her heart pounding. "I just thought of something. What if that unstable dynamite is around here?"

"Yeah!" Ruby breathed the word. "Jack said any loud noise could set it off and blow ever'thing to kingdom come."

"Well," Spud replied, "it must not be too close or those two cars wrecking would have—"

"Shh!" Hildy interrupted. "I hear voices again."

All three listened briefly, then Hildy whispered, "They're up where that car came from. And they're coming this way. Let's go!"

"Whar we a-goin'?" Ruby asked in a small, frightened voice.

"Back to the ladder. Maybe the deputies are there by now and they can handle this." Hildy led the way, her light bouncing ahead as she ran. "Faster! Faster!"

She heard Ruby and Spud pounding along on her heels as the passage behind her took on a pale glow, like dawn breaking. It took Hildy a moment to realize what it was.

"Lights!" she said aloud, glancing back. "It's lights from the hats of whoever's chasing us." She tripped as she spoke and almost fell.

"Don't talk!" Spud cried. "Just look where you're going, and keep running."

Hildy nodded, breathing hard both from fear and the effort

of running. At the curve where the two ore cars had jumped the tracks, she had to stop to pick her way around the rocks the second car had strewn. She glanced back.

"Those men are still coming," she announced. "But they're not running."

"I wonder why not?" Spud asked, easing around the debris. "Unless—?"

"Unless they think there's no hurry because we can't escape," Hildy finished his thought aloud.

Ruby moaned. "They got us jist like they got pore ol' Jack!"

Hildy slowed enough to look back again. The pursuers were falling behind. Their lights barely showed the wrecked ore cars.

"We're going to make it," Spud puffed. "I think the big stope's just ahead, and the ladder's not much farther."

Seconds later, Hildy glanced briefly into the big stope as she ran past it. Her light showed the huge boulder she had noticed before. Ruby's light crisscrossed hers as she also looked into the excavation.

Ruby stopped suddenly. "Lookee yonder!"

"What?" Hildy asked in sudden alarm, halting so abruptly that Spud almost bumped into her. At the same instant, her light focused where Ruby's was.

At first, Hildy saw only the boulder and the room itself. The left wall was only about four feet high, telling her that the Cornishmen who had labored there with hammers and drills had to sit or crouch. Three round timbers a foot or more in diameter and about four feet long supported the low stone ceiling at that point. Then it rose steeply, so that a tall person could stand upright. From the apex, the ceiling slanted off to the right, again requiring stout timbers to support it at the wall.

All three lights focused on the immense boulder. It was half the size of an automobile, well back and slightly to the right of the stope's center. Next to the boulder Hildy saw the wooden box and the terrifying word: EXPLOSIVES.

She stood in petrified stillness, seeing sticks of dynamite both inside the box and lying around on the rocky ground. Little beads on the sticks reflected the light like countless evil amber eyes.

Hildy whispered, "It's the sweating dynamite Jack told us about!"

"An' over yonder's somethin' else!" Ruby's voice shot up. "Jist past that rock. It's a laig! A human—"

Fearfully, Hildy took a couple of quick steps so her light shone behind the boulder. "It's Jack!" she cried.

The boy lay on his back, eyes closed, his left leg twisted at a strange angle. His hard hat lay beside him, the light extinguished.

Ruby whispered, "Is he—daid?"

Hearing the pursuers' voices growing closer, Hildy quickly knelt by Jack and felt his wrist for a pulse.

—

CHAPTER Nineteen

TRAPPED DEEP IN
THE MINE

Saturday Morning

Quickly Hildy shifted her fingers on Jack's limp wrist, making sure she was touching the place where the artery should be. *There's no pulse!*

Hildy started to look up and shake her head in despair when her right forefinger felt something.

"Wait!" she whispered, focusing her light on the wrist. "I feel a pulse! He's alive!"

"He is?" Spud exclaimed. He bent over the unconscious boy and felt his wrist. "You're right!"

"But he cain't go noplace like that," Ruby said hoarsely. "An' them voices is a-gittin' closer ever' second. What're we a-gonna do?"

"I'm thinking," Hildy replied. "I'm thinking."

Spud's light moved up to Jack's forehead. "Look. See that bump on his right temple? He probably lost his hat when he dived in here, trying to get away from the first ore car, and he hit his head on that boulder."

"Don't stand thar a-talkin'!" Ruby said. "Thar ain't time!"

Hildy's fear of closed places receded in sudden concern for the safety of everyone. She knew their pursuers were still coming, but the light of their carbide lamps was only a faint glow. They had to be some distance up the inclined passage. They came slowly, but purposefully, as if knowing they now had time, because their quarry could not escape.

Spud's voice made Hildy snap her attention back to Jack. "I don't think his leg's broken, but he wouldn't be able to stand on it even if he was conscious."

"We can't leave him!" she exclaimed. "Let's see if we can carry him."

"We cain't do that," Ruby protested. "He's too heavy! An' I hear them men a-gittin' closer. We air gonna git ketched fer shore!"

"Don't argue!" Spud said sharply. "Give us a hand. Let's see if we can get him out of here."

Ruby dropped to her knees before Jack's feet, and reached to grip his ankles. "Don't nobody make no sudden noise now and make that ol' dynamite go off!"

Reminded of the danger, Hildy glanced at the sweating dynamite sticks. The amber droplets seemed to wink mockingly at her. She tore her gaze from the dangerous powder and grabbed Jack's right hand.

"Spud, if you take one arm, I'll take the other; Ruby has his feet—"

"Do it!" Spud commanded, reaching down. "If we can't lift him, we'll drag him. Ready?"

"Ready," Ruby and Hildy replied together.

"Lift!"

Hildy hadn't thought about her sore shoulder until she tried to straighten up. Excruciating pain hit so hard she sagged to her knees, almost dropping Jack's arm.

"What's the matter?" Spud asked anxiously.

"I forgot about my arm. It was almost pulled out of the socket when the ladder rung broke. But it'll be all right. Let's try again."

"Maybe Ruby and I can drag him," Spud said.

Hildy glanced toward the passage, suddenly aware of a change. "They've stopped!"

Spud looked up. "The men?"

"Yes, listen."

All three stood in tense silence.

Finally Hildy said softly, "They're not coming any more; they're doing something else. Hear it? I can't quite make it out, but it sounds like sawing."

"It's a saw, all right," Spud replied. "They're cutting something."

"What fer?" Ruby asked. "If they's a-chasin' us, and got us whar we cain't git away—"

"I know what it is!" Hildy interrupted, her heart galloping. "They're sawing through timber. When it's cut in two, it'll collapse, letting the rocks fall . . ." She stopped, shuddering, unwilling to say what would happen next.

Spud finished for her, "And that'll shake the ground so hard the dynamite will go off! This whole place will—"

"Don't say it!" Ruby broke in. "Maybe if'n we run real fast, draggin' Jack—but how kin we git back up—?"

"Ohhhh!" A low moan cut her off.

Hildy glanced down at Jack. His eyes blinked open, then closed again.

"He's coming to!" Hildy exclaimed, dropping to her knees beside the boy's head. "Jack, Jack! Can you hear me?"

Jack squinted and raised his right hand to cover his eyes. "I hear you, but I can't see behind those lights. Who is it?"

"It's me—Hildy. With Ruby and Spud. We're going to get you out of here."

Slowly, Jack started to sit up, then let out a groan. "Oh, my leg!" He reached out and clutched it with both hands just above the knee. "I just remembered—!"

"Tell us later!" Hildy cried. "If we get you to your feet, can you stand up?"

"Stop a-talkin' and let's git him up!" Ruby cried. "Only this time me'n Spud'll do it ourselves. I'll take this arm. Spud, ye take t'other. Hildy, lead the way so's we kin see good."

Hildy nodded reluctantly.

Seconds later, Jack was standing, one arm over Ruby's shoulder, the other over Spud's.

"It hurts like blazes," Jack announced, grimacing in pain. "But if you'll let me lean on you—"

"Lean away," Spud instructed. "Let's go, Ruby."

"Ye don't need to tell me what to do," she replied tartly. "I kin hear them men a-sawin' same's you kin."

"Sawing?" Jack asked as he hobbled on his good right leg, supported between Ruby and Spud. "Oh, I hear it." He sucked in his breath sharply, his voice thin, sounding frightened. "You know what they're doing?"

"We know," Hildy said grimly, moving toward the entrance to the passage. "Probably the same thing they did to your father."

Her glance showed that the three pursuers' carbide lamps were pointed upward, revealing a heavy squared overhead timber supported by one on either side. Together, the three timbers made an inverted U. The saw blade flashed silver streaks of light as it ripped through the top center of the overhead beam.

"Let's go!" Spud's urgent command broke Hildy's terrified but fascinated gaze.

"It's a big timber," Jack said, limping along down the passage toward the ladder. "It'll take them a few minutes to cut through it."

"Long enough fer us to git up that thar ladder?" Ruby asked hopefully.

"Who knows?" Jack replied, puffing with the exertion of hobbling on one leg. "Maybe all of you had better leave me and save yourselves."

"Don't talk like that!" Hildy said firmly. "We're all going to make it."

"Thanks," Jack said with feeling. "But you shouldn't have come down here."

"Neither should you have," Hildy reminded him. "You were supposed to wait for us up above."

"I came here early and fixed the ladder," Jack explained, "I climbed back up to the surface to wait for the deputies when I heard tapping from below—"

"Haints!" Ruby exclaimed, her voice high and shrill. "Ye heered them little whatchamacallems, didn't ye?"

"Not tommyknockers," Jack said, the hobbling making his voice tremble. "I know, because when I stuck my head into the shaft again, I heard voices. Men's voices. So I took my hammer and came back down."

"Voices?" Hildy asked, glancing fearfully back toward where the saw was still ripping through the overhead timber. "Whose voices?"

"Who do you think? Garrett Kayne, Casper Cobb, and somebody else."

Hildy sucked in her breath. "You sure?"

"I'm sure! I couldn't make out who the third man was. I tried to follow them, but they ambushed me with an ore car."

"We found it," Hildy said, trying to stave off the rising sense of urgency generated by the incessant sound of the saw behind them.

"They tried to git us with another car," Ruby added. "When that didn't work, they follered us an' then went to work a-cuttin' with that thar ol' saw."

Hildy's light showed Jack's left leg still twisted outward. He started talking so fast Hildy guessed he was trying to cover up his fear and pain with a torrent of words.

"It's a good thing my leg was okay when that ore car came shooting down the drift toward me. Those guys cut the cable, but I heard the car coming and started running.

"Made it to that stope and dived in just before I heard the car jump the track at the curve. If it had hit me, it would have smashed me like a bug. As it was, I tripped on the rail, diving head first in there. Twisted my leg and lost my hat, so the light went out. Must've cracked my head on that boulder. Knocked me out."

Ruby asked, "Jack, air ye a-gonna be able to climb that thar ladder on jist one foot?"

"I'll manage," he said grimly. "If we can just get there before that timber's cut in two."

"We'll get there." Hildy turned to look back, her light showing how far they'd come from the stope.

"How kin ye be so shore?" Ruby asked anxiously.

"Those men can't cut that overhead piece of wood all the way through, or it'd come down before they could get back the other way to safety," Hildy explained. "So my guess is that they'll cut it to what they judge a safe point, then run."

"That makes sense," Jack agreed. "The weakened timber will eventually give way, making lots of noise and setting off a small earthquake. That'll make the unstable dynamite go off. That's what they must have done to my father."

Ruby asked in a scared whisper, "Will that ol' timber hold long enough fer us to git up that ladder?"

A shiver rippled over Hildy's shoulders. She forced her mind away from their terrible jeopardy. Leading the way toward the ladder in the shaft, she tried to understand how their pursuers had known where they'd be this morning. Her mind raced back to what Jack had said.

Three men—Garrett Kayne, Casper Cobb and . . . who else? Not Trey, he's home with his wife. So who's the third person? Oh, I know! Probably the truck driver who chased us off the dump. What was his name? Rasor? Or maybe it was his swamper. But how'd they know Jack was going to be here this morning?

A strange, creepy-crawly feeling made gooseflesh ripple down Hildy's arms.

Behind her, Ruby asked, "Kin ye go faster, Jack?"

"I'm not used to hobbling like this, especially when my leg is killing me, but I'm trying as hard as I can."

"We'll make it," Hildy assured them absently, still preoccupied with her thoughts as she led the way along the tracks toward the mine shaft.

Why did those men try to run Jack down with that ore car? It has to be because they knew he had talked with Trey, and that Jack was going to lead the deputies down here to see the place where his father was killed.

Hildy frowned, remembering what had troubled her before. *How did Trey know my name?*

Her thoughts were interrupted by Jack's voice. "Just a little bit more to the ladder. We should be able to see it soon. What's that?"

Hildy stopped instantly, her ears filling with a strange new sound from just ahead. She tried to pierce the darkness with her light. "It sounds like . . . a landslide!"

"The shaft!" Jack's words were barely audible. "It's caving in!"

Hildy moaned in sudden despair. "Oh, no!"

There was no doubt Jack was right. Hildy heard the unmistakable sound of rocks and dirt sliding downhill. She had a mental picture of the shaft collapsing, the ladder being swept away and buried under the shifting mound of debris.

The dynamite! Hildy whirled around, her light bouncing off the passage behind them. *Was the noise enough to cause an explosion?*

Far behind, where the pursuers' lights made a faint glowing circle, Hildy heard another sound—the creaking of timber starting to give away.

A voice came through the darkness. "That's enough! Let's get out of here!"

The lights turned away, and total blackness settled in the drift behind. A faint smell of dust made Hildy pivot to look ahead.

"It's stopped," Spud said in an awed voice. "The landslide's stopped. But did it completely close the shaft so we can't get out?"

Hildy breathed a silent prayer while the weakened overhead timber behind them sent out a cracking sound as it slowly gave way under the tons of overhead rock.

Her claustrophobia returned in a violent rush, causing her heart to pound so fast it seemed about to explode.

For a long moment, she stood with the others in total silence, caught between the danger behind and the one ahead.

Ruby finally whispered, "We're plumb trapped! Thar ain't no way out!"

CHAPTER TWENTY

THE MINE BLOWS UP

Late Saturday Morning

Hildy whirled around, the light from her hissing carbide lamp striking Ruby full in the face. "Don't talk like that!" Hildy said firmly. "We're alive, so we've still got a chance, but we've got to keep our heads!"

Ruby took a slow breath, then let it out. "I'm plumb sorry. What kin we do?"

"Yeah," Jack said, still leaning on Ruby and Spud's shoulders. "What *can* we do?"

Hildy looked around, her thoughts tumbling over each other. There were two choices—both of them bad.

One was to try rushing back toward the weakening overhead beam in hopes of getting beyond it before it collapsed and set off the dynamite.

That won't work, Hildy told herself. *There's no way we could get Jack past it in time. So that leaves only the shaft—if it's not completely closed by the landslide. Even if it's open, we have only a little time to get up to the surface. And with Jack's bad leg. . . .*

"Well?" Ruby asked. "Ye gonna jist stand thar?"

Hildy turned toward the shaft. "Follow me!"

She could hear Jack hobbling along, with Ruby and Spud urging him on. Behind them, the overhead timber creaked and groaned with rising frequency and intensity.

There was no doubt in Hildy's mind that when the beam broke, the unstable nitroglycerin in the old dynamite would explode. The entire passage would collapse under countless tons of quartz and granite.

She prayed, fervently and silently, as her light slowly drove back the darkness. Every step brought her closer to the station where miners long ago had removed and delivered materials by the shaft that rose to the surface. She saw that the landslide had originated in the shaft, spilling out into the station. Bits of dust still hung in the air, reflecting her light like headlights in fog. A few pieces of rock slid down the larger pile that marked the location of the avalanche.

Then Hildy saw something else, and her heart almost stopped. "O Lord," Hildy whispered. "No!"

The ladder that offered escape to safety above was torn away from its moorings. It lay in broken sections on top of the steep pile.

"We're goners!" Ruby whispered, her light blending with Hildy's and Spud's on the destruction ahead.

Hildy raised her eyes, sending the rays of her carbide lamp upward. "Look!" the word erupted from her mouth. "Daylight! The top of the shaft is still open."

"Yeah, but just barely," Spud said. "There's room for only one person at a time to squeeze through."

"We can make it!" Hildy replied.

"An' our daddies air up thar!" Ruby exclaimed, sudden hope lifting her voice, "an' that powder monkey, an' maybe dep'ties. They'll have ropes and sich like. But . . ." her voice weakened and trailed off.

"No buts!" Hildy broke in. "Let's see if we can climb up this slide." She turned back, remembering Jack. "Do you think you can make it with that bad leg?"

"Well, I'm sure not going to stand here and die without

trying," the boy said. "Maybe if one of you climbed up above and pulled, and somebody pushed from below—"

"Spud, you and Ruby go up," Hildy interrupted. "I can't pull with this sore shoulder, but I can push on his feet from below, or at least keep him from sliding back."

In seconds Ruby and Spud had started scrambling up the pile of rubble. At first Hildy didn't think it was going to work, because some heavy rocks came loose and crashed to the passageway floor, causing both Ruby and Spud to slip back. But as Hildy held her breath, the two stopped sliding, found secure footing, and bent to reach down for Jack's upstretched hands.

Using his good right leg, the miner's son shoved himself upward toward them. Gingerly, Hildy tried pushing on the sole of Jack's other boot.

He let out a moan. "Don't!" he cried in pain. "It hurts too much!"

For a moment, everyone stopped, their lamps lighting up the precarious scene.

Jack said, "It's no use! I can't make it. The rest of you go on before it's too late."

"No!" Hildy cried. "Look! On top. They're lowering ropes." She raised her voice. "Daddy, Uncle Nate, hurry! This whole thing's going to blow up any minute!"

From far above, a man's voice called back faintly. "We'll have you out in a jiffy. Ropes are coming down."

Four ropes suddenly appeared in the circle of light made by the three carbide lamps. Spud and Jack let out a rousing yell of joy and hope. Ruby gave a little sob of relief. Hildy's lips moved in a silent prayer of gratitude. She broke it off suddenly as the ropes stopped dropping.

"They're too short!" she exclaimed. "We've got to climb higher to reach them. Hurry! Hurry!"

Desperately, knowing the terrible consequences of any further delay, Hildy, Ruby, Spud, and Jack struggled upward. Their feet dislodged rocks, sending them crashing into the darkness below.

Jack said through clenched teeth, "Don't worry about hurting me. Push, pull, shove—whatever it takes."

It seemed to take forever, and Hildy's mind retreated from the awful reality of how little time there was and what a long distance was left. She inched upward, methodically, shoving against Jack's boot while trying to climb with her free hand.

Ruby mumbled, "When I git outta this, I'm a-gonna snatch them bal'headed fer doin' this to us—whoever they be!"

Hildy's mind grasped at the thought of escaping to unmask the one who had masterminded the plan that took the life of John Tremayne and had set up this second fatal "accident."

We know who everyone is except the ringleader, Hildy told herself, *But who is that?*

She kept climbing, ignoring her bleeding fingers and skinned knees caused by the rough rocks. Her mind escaped the present terrifying situation to safer thoughts.

Garrett Kayne, Casper Cobb, and the others may not go to prison for highgrading, but they will for causing Jack's father's death—and for trying to kill us. But who's the leader? And how did Trey know my name?

"Oh!" Hildy exclaimed aloud as the answer hit her. All the little nagging problems that had plagued her before were gone. All the questions that had robbed her of peace were answered.

Jack asked, "What'd you say?"

"I know who's behind all this!" Hildy cried, confidence making her voice loud and strong.

"Me, too!" Jack answered, his voice showing he was obviously suffering a lot of pain. "The ones who cut that timber below and chased me! Garrett Kayne and Casper Cobb—and whoever the third man is."

"Trey Granger," Spud added.

"No!" Hildy said, shoving on Jack's foot again, her mind clear and racing with hope. "Trey was involved at first, but changed his mind and wanted out after Jack's father was killed."

"Then who was the third man down there this morning?" Jack asked, puffing hard from the exertion and pain.

Ruby snapped, "Don't talk now! Jist climb! That ol' piece of wood's liable to bust any secont."

Hildy kept on, but her mind spun with excitement. She knew who that person was. *But will we get out of here alive so I can tell?*

"The ropes!" Spud yelled. "I've got one! Ruby, grab that one while I get the other two. There—we've got all four!"

"Quick!" Hildy yelled up. "Get one under Jack's shoulders. Hurry, hurry!"

From far below Hildy was sure she heard the distant thump of a rock as it fell from the collapsing timber. She involuntarily flinched and sucked in her breath, wondering if she would hear the explosion that would claim her life.

"What're you doing, Hildy?" Spud's voice broke into her thoughts. "Grab the rope! Tie it under your arms like the rest of us. We're ready to go up."

"I'm tying," Hildy called, slipping the rope's end under her armpits. At the same time, she cringed against the expected blast from below. "Ready!" she cried, tying a quick knot across her chest.

Spud called upward through the remaining narrow shaft, "Pull us up! Pull! Pull!"

"Yeah!" Ruby yelled. "Pull!"

Seconds later, Hildy saw Ruby, Spud, and Jack lifted, foot by precious foot. Then Hildy's own rope tightened, and she felt herself moving up across broken rocks. They cut, gouged, scraped, and tore, but were nothing compared to what she knew was going to happen if the dynamite blew up before she reached the top of the shaft.

Hildy wanted to close her eyes, but she kept them open to help guide her way through the narrow opening. The darkness gave way to increasing light until Hildy could see anxious faces peering down from the surface.

"I'm out!" Spud called, scrambling over the collar of the shaft. Hildy saw him leap to his feet and reach down to grab Ruby's rope. "Hurry! Hurry!" he shouted to the men whose arms moved rapidly, pulling on the three remaining ropes.

"I made it!" Ruby shouted a moment later.

Far below, in the darkness behind her, Hildy was sure she heard more rocks falling faster and faster. She closed her eyes, but couldn't shut out the sound.

Too late! her mind screamed. *They'll never get Jack and me out in time!*

In her mind's eye, she could see the sawed overhead timber in the passageway slowly cracking. It gave way, inch by inch, allowing small rocks to fall, then more and more as the timber rapidly approached the breaking point.

"Get her out!" Jack's voice made Hildy open her eyes. "This whole thing's going to blow up any second!"

Hildy glanced up. The miner's son was on his knees at the opening to the shaft. He reached down to pull on the remaining rope, which already had many hands grasping it.

Slowly, ever so slowly, it seemed to Hildy, she was borne upward. She saw her father's frightened face. Then his strong hands gripped her wrists.

A second later she was in his arms. He clutched her close like a little child. He whirled and ran awkwardly away from the shaft before setting her down. "Run, everybody!" he yelled. "Run!"

Hildy saw everyone running and shouting. It was like a blur, but she made out her uncle Nate, Ben Strong, Red Barnes, Ruby, and Spud. Two uniformed sheriff's deputies were supporting Jack between them as he hobbled, almost falling, toward the line of ponderosas. Someone else was running ahead of them all, but Hildy couldn't tell who it was.

Suddenly, the ground trembled and wobbled drunkenly, throwing Hildy off her feet. She saw some of the other runners go down, and some stagger, trying to keep their balance.

"Whump!" The muffled sound behind Hildy made her whirl around in time to see the mine shaft erupt in a grayish-black geyser.

"Down!" the powder monkey cried. "Everybody down! Cover your heads with your hands!"

Hildy instinctively obeyed, closing her eyes and rolling herself into a tight ball. She heard bits of rock and debris fall around her. A small rock smashed into her left ankle, and smaller pieces peppered her body and arms.

She didn't know how long she lay there, curled up tightly, silently praying, but she was aware that the rain of rocks and other debris had stopped. She opened her eyes and raised up slightly.

Red Barnes got to his feet and glanced around. "Everyone okay?"

Hildy quickly checked herself and was relieved to see nothing more serious than a bruise on her ankle and the cuts and scrapes she had received in the mine. She glanced around and saw that everyone else was all right.

Ruby let out a happy yell. "Didja think we'd live to be a-sittin' here like this, all safe an' sound?"

Slowly Hildy got to her feet, so glad to be alive that she felt like shouting. Instead, she grabbed Ruby and gave her a big hug. Everyone else seemed to be hugging someone, with the men thumping each other on the back and talking loudly, congratulating each other.

Even Ruby and Spud turned toward each other, paused in awkward uncertainty, then hugged each other.

Hildy turned toward the place where the mine shaft had been. Out of the corner of her eye, she saw all the others do the same. They stood in awed silence.

The opening was gone, completely closed. The earth around it for several feet had sunk in upon it, making a shallow depression. Little puffs of dust still rose into the air. There was the occasional sound of rocks settling.

Ruby broke the silence from where she stood in front of her tall father, his arms encircling her. "Jist a few minutes ago in that thar ol' mine, I figgered for shore we was all goners!"

Hildy's father stood with his right arm around her shoulder. "We should never have let you kids go down there in the first place."

"If you hadn't," Jack said, standing on his right leg, the left one lifted up behind him, "I'd be dead."

He began telling what had happened to him before Hildy, Ruby, and Spud arrived. They joined in, recounting the events after that.

When they had finished, the taller of the two deputies cleared his throat. "We'll pick up Kayne and Cobb. But who was the third man down there?"

Jack shrugged. "I couldn't tell."

"Maybe the truck driver, Rasor," Hildy guessed. "Or his swamper."

Jack looked at Hildy. "I thought you said you knew who the ringleader was."

Hildy felt all eyes turn toward her. "I was trying to keep from thinking about the awful thing that was going to happen to us, so I made myself think of other things.

"For the last day or so, I've kept asking myself, 'What am I overlooking?' And then last night and this morning I wondered, 'How did Trey know my name?' Suddenly, it all came to me, and I knew."

"Knew what?" Ruby demanded impatiently.

"I knew who was behind this highgrading and caused the death of Jack's father. What's more, I knew his motive."

"Hildy!" Ruby cried impatiently. "Tell us! Who?"

Hildy looked around the circle of everyone present, including the person she'd seen running away ahead of the others just before the mine blew up.

"There," Hildy said, pointing. "There he is!"

CHAPTER
TWENTY-ONE

WHEN PUZZLE
PIECES FIT

Saturday Afternoon

Hildy heard startled exclamations as Ruby leaned close and whispered, "Hildy, ye gone plumb daft?"

Hildy lowered her accusing finger. She glanced around the circle, looking into the eyes of her father, her cousin, her uncle, Spud, the old ranger, the powder monkey, the two deputies, and Jack. Everyone showed the same disbelief that Ruby had expressed.

"I'd better explain," Hildy began. "I kept wondering how Trey Granger knew my name, because only four people in this town knew it. Three of them didn't have a motive for threatening me. They were Jack, Mrs. Callahan, and Skeezix. That left only one other person who knew my name. That's you, Mr. Cowan."

The mine superintendent cried indignantly, "That's ridiculous, Hildy!"

"Is it?" she asked. "I knew that whoever was behind all this had to have more power than Garrett Kayne, Casper Cobb, or Trey Granger. It had to be somebody who was above suspicion, someone who could hire people and place them where he wanted in the mine. Or even hire a pilot to fly stolen gold from here to Mexico. Since Trey's a pilot, that's how he got involved, isn't it?"

"You're talking nonsense!" Cowan said sharply. "If I were guilty of what you say, why would I be here?"

"Because," Hildy said evenly, "somebody in the police or sheriff's office who owes you a favor called to say what was going to happen here this morning."

"More nonsense!" he snapped. "I'm here because I just found out that John Tremayne had left written orders for this old shaft to be blown up by today. I just came by to see if it was done."

"I think you came because you wanted to be sure whoever went into this mine shaft didn't come out," Hildy said quietly. "You wanted to be sure an 'accident' here stopped anybody from talking—or being suspicious—the same as you did in the case of Jack's father. Then you could go on with your highgrading."

Leith Cowan turned imploringly to the others. "All of you know she's talking crazy, don't you?"

Before anyone could answer, Hildy rushed on. "You were getting rich, stealing from the Shasta Daisy, but somehow Jack's father found out. He threatened to expose you to the mine owner. You couldn't allow that, so you arranged for Jack's father to die in what looked like a mining accident."

The mine superintendent turned to Hildy's father. "You'd better stop your daughter before I sue you and her for slandering my good name!"

"I want to hear what she has to say," her father replied. "Go on, Hildy."

Hildy continued. "It took me a long time to figure it out, but it finally came. You see, Jack told me that his father threatened to go to the mine *owner*. That kept bothering me, because it seemed logical that Mr. Tremayne would have gone to *his* boss, the mine superintendent—you, Mr. Cowan. Finally, I realized that Jack's father couldn't do that because *you* were the one he was going to turn in to *your* boss. That's Mr. Farnham."

Cowan said coolly, "Nobody'll believe such a wild story. Why, I'm a member of the church and half the civic and fraternal organizations in this town. You're just a crazy kid!"

The tall deputy stepped forward to face Cowan. "They don't have to believe her. We have Trey Granger's sworn statement, naming you, Leith Cowan, as the principal responsible for the murder of John Tremayne. Granger also named three other accomplices, including Casper Cobb, a truck driver named Rasor, and his swamper, name of Hampton.

"Warrants have already been issued for their arrest. They'll probably cop a plea in order to save their own necks, and that'll mean four peoples' word against yours. My partner and I were going directly from here to your office, but we were delayed because of the emergency here. Leith Cowan, you're under arrest for suspected highgrading and murder."

"Add attempted murder to that charge," the old ranger said, "for what almost happened to these four youngsters this morning."

As the protesting mine superintendent was led away, Hildy's father put his arm around her shoulder. "Our deadline's up, and we've done what we came for. Let's all go home."

Later that afternoon, Ben drove the yellow Packard toward Lone River with the three young people and other two men inside.

Ruby said, "I jist cain't see how ye figgered all that out, Hildy. What putcha onto Mr. Cowan?"

"Well, I realized early on that whoever was trying to scare us off knew an awful lot about who we were and why we were here."

Spud said, "I certainly wouldn't have suspected Leith Cowan."

"Me either," Hildy admitted. "Although we didn't tell Mr. Cowan exactly why we were here, he could easily figure it out, because Mr. Farnham called him and told him to cooperate with us in whatever we wanted.

"So the gang started out by trying to scare us off. When that didn't work—not even when those two men roughed you up, Uncle Nate—I figured it was only a matter of time until they tried something desperate."

"Which they done," Ruby said somberly. "An' almost done us all in!"

"Another thing that helped my thinking," Hildy went on, "was when Ruby and I saw Garrett Kayne carrying a sack of gold up to that big white house where he was supposed to live. But that didn't make sense until I learned he'd recently moved from there. Then I knew he and Trey—and probably Casper Cobb—were leaving sacks of gold for the man who now lived there."

"That's Leith Cowan," the old ranger put in. "After I left all of you last night, I found out that Garrett Kayne had recently moved from that house, and Cowan now occupied it. Kayne was leaving one of those sacks of gold-bearing ore on Cowan's front porch the night Kayne saw you girls."

"That's what I finally figured out," Hildy agreed. "By giving Cowan part of what they'd stolen from the mine, Mr. Kayne and the others were paying him so they could steal more for themselves. But he was double-crossing them too. In fact, what the gang members got was small stuff compared to what Mr. Cowan was doing for himself. He stole an occasional gold bar or two from the refinery and had Trey fly the ingots to Mexico so they could be sold on the world market."

Spud said, "Hildy, if you hadn't made the connection between the airport and Trey being a pilot, we might have watched forever for gold to be shipped by rail."

She nodded her thanks to Spud. "There was a third way Mr. Cowan was involved in highgrading, but it took me a while to figure that out. You see, I wondered why Jack, Ruby, and I were allowed to pick up around the mine dump one day, but the next day, that truck driver and his swamper drove us off. Finally I remembered that we'd seen an ore car from the mine empty a load at the dump just minutes before the truck driver showed up."

"Oh, I git it!" Ruby cried. "Some o' them cars didn't jist have waste rock. They had rocks with gold in 'em. Then I reckon the truck driver took that load somewhars to another stamp mill, whar they crushed out the gold an' didn't ask no questions!"

The old ranger said, "Most highgraders got away with only a few nuggets or gold-bearing quartz that they sneaked out of the mine. Cowan's greed did him in."

Hildy's Uncle Nate explained, "Young Jack told me he's going to stop picking up gold at the dump after school. Says he doesn't want to do anything that even looks like highgrading, even though now he doesn't know how he'll help support his widowed mother and his little sisters and brothers."

Ben said, "Don't worry about that. I know Matt Farnham well enough to know he'll see to it that Jack and his family are taken care of for his help in this case."

Ruby said, "Nobody's 'splained to me what that tappin' was when we was a-lookin' fer Jack. He said he didn't do it. Ye reckon they is sich things as tommyknockers?"

Spud looked thoughtful. "I've been thinking about that. There's a possible scientific explanation. We know sound travels farther over water than through the air, so why couldn't sound carry long distances through hard rocks like granite or quartz?"

Ruby scoffed. "Thar ye go a-gin with yore high an' mighty idees! Why, I'd jist as soon think some outlaws was hidin' out down there, and they done the tappin'."

Spud shook his head. "Ruby, you know nobody in his right mind would stay down in that section of the mine; it's too dangerous."

Ruby flared, "Then it was them tommyknockers!" She turned to Hildy. "Don't ye reckon that's so?"

Hildy paused a moment, thinking hard. "Whatever it was," she said finally, "it was God's way of warning us."

Everyone was thoughtfully silent. Hildy glanced at all three men, then Spud and Ruby. There were gentle nods from all.

Ben said in his soft drawl, "Yep! Makes sense, Hildy."

Spud changed the subject. "Hildy, you sure used your head on this whole thing."

"I just wanted to help stop the highgrading from Mr. Farnham's mine so he could build that hospital."

"He'll build it," the old ranger assured her. "Too bad your classmate had to die, but the new hospital will save a lot of lives in the future."

Hildy felt good about that although she was still sad for Gladys Cassell. "Maybe if I'd thought of what the Bible says about looking on the heart as God does, instead of on the outside as people do, we might not have had the close call we did today."

"That's true," her uncle said softly. "But remember that if we hadn't all come up here, Trey wouldn't have been able to talk to me when he needed someone who could help him make the right decisions about the Lord and helping the police."

"That's right," Ben Strong said. "But there are two other things you need to think about."

"What are they?" Hildy asked.

"Before we left Lone River, Matt told me he'd give a cash reward to everyone if we solved this case fast."

Hildy looked up expectantly. "You think it'll be enough that I can buy Molly that $15 wooden washing machine?"

"Maybe even a better one than that," the old ranger replied with a smile. "Ruby can get her bike too."

The cousins grinned happily at each other.

"That's one thing," Spud said to the driver. "What's the other one?"

"The law-enforcement agencies think there really is a plot underway to rob the gold train."

"No kidding?" Spud exclaimed. "Nobody's done that in the sixty-five years it's been carrying gold!"

"Well, police informants say somebody's about to try it. They've asked me to come back and work on the case with them. We hope to prevent the robbery and catch the responsibles before somebody gets hurt."

"Oh, boy!" Spud exclaimed. "I'd sure like to help!"

"Me, too," Ruby said.

Hildy nodded. "That'd be wonderful. Then we could all see Skeezix and Jack again. But we can't, because we have to return to school."

"Maybe they won't git that ol' gas leak finished fer a while," Ruby said hopefully, "an we kin come back here."

"Don't count on it, honey," her father commented.

Hildy leaned over and touched her cousin's arm. "Regardless of whether we get back to Quartz City or not, you know we always find something exciting wherever we are."

"Or something exciting finds you," Spud said with a wide grin.

Ruby opened her mouth as though to make a smart remark, then she also grinned. "Reckon yo're right fer once, Spud."

They all laughed as the Packard continued toward Lone River and whatever adventures lay ahead.